Secrets Before Supper

The Wronged Women's Co-operative: Book 10

T E SCOTT

Copyright © 2024 T E Scott

All rights reserved.

ISBN: 9798340315793

Chapter 1: Bernie

Bernie Paterson stared at the sobbing woman on the other side of the desk and tried to feel some sort of sympathy. It wasn't that Bernie was incapable of the emotion. Despite what most people who met her assumed, she was able to feel pity. When she had worked at the care home she had experienced sympathy every day for families who had lost loved ones to death or dementia. At the same time, Bernie had learned how to work through those pangs of sympathy and keep her manner efficient and professional. If people saw her as cold, that was their problem.

However, when Bernie was trying to get information out of someone and they kept dissolving into snottery, wailing sobs, it simply became an irritation. Every gram of pity that Bernie possessed had been used up within five minutes of meeting Kaylie-Ann Michelson.

"Sorry," Kaylie snuffled into her tissue. "It's just all so dreadful. I spent two grand on that wedding dress and now it's all for nothing."

"You spent two thousand pounds on a dress?" Bernie didn't even try to keep the contempt from her voice.

"Aye. Well, my dad paid for it. It's tradition, isn't it?"

Before Bernie could tell her just what she thought of that

particular tradition, the woman had started wailing once more.

"At least he didn't leave you at the altar," Bernie said in a gap between sobs.

"I wouldn't have cared so much. At least then I would have got to wear the dress. It had Swarovski crystals. And the veil was ten feet long."

Another flood of sobs. Bernie had had enough.

"What exactly is it you want us to find out?"

"Why he dumped me of course!" Kaylie glared at her like it was obvious. "Two weeks before the wedding. There's got to be a reason."

"A reason or a person?" Bernie asked.

Kaylie-Ann stopped crying for a moment. "Ryan wouldn't cheat on me. He says there's no one else and I believe him."

Bernie didn't feel the need to mention that if men were telling the truth when they said there 'wasn't anyone else' then the entire business model of their private investigation agency would have failed on day one.

"What reason did he give you for breaking it off?"

"He said it wasn't the right time. That he was having 'doubts'. I mean, he wasn't having doubts when we were getting our matching tattoos, was he?"

Oh bloody hell.

"It won't be cheap," Bernie said, deciding to stick to the facts. "I mean, we'll have to do some surveillance. Find out who he's meeting up with."

"He's not seeing someone else."

"Of course he isn't," Bernie said, not even trying to sound sincere. "Why do you think he dumped you then?"

"I reckon it's that mother of his," Kaylie said, the hatred clear in her voice. "Nasty old woman. She never liked me. Said I'd had botox!"

Bernie tried not to look at the woman's forehead. "And you haven't?"

"Only a bit of lip fillers."

"Right."

Bernie pushed her contract across the desk. "We'll need a five hundred pound deposit to start with. But costs will be higher than that."

"Whatever it takes," Kaylie sniffed. "I just want him back."

"Uh huh. You don't want to get a dog or something? A hell of a lot easier to look after than a man and definitely more loyal."

"You're joking, right?"

Why were people always asking her that? Bernie simply shrugged in reply. Kaylie signed the form and transferred the money using her phone into the WWC account.

"I'll be in touch in a couple of days," Bernie told her as Kaylie made her way out of the door. She watched as her new client climbed into a sparkling clean white Mini Cooper and wondered if dad had paid for that one too. Bernie shook her head. No doubt the young lad had been shagging around, but at least it would be an easy case to solve.

Once Kaylie had driven away, Bernie turned back to the front door. The new brass sign had a tiny smudge on one side. Bernie huffed on it and gave it a rub with her sleeve. Perfect. She read it one more time with the same proud feeling as when they had first put it up.

The Wronged Women's Co-operative, Number 1 Private Investigators in Invergryff.

As the other members of her team had pointed out, they were also the only private investigators in Invergryff, but that didn't make the sign any less true. What had once been an average semi-detached house on an unremarkable street was now the HQ of a detective agency famous throughout the land. Or this part of Renfrewshire at the very least.

Bernie's phone started to buzz.

"Hello?"

"Were you nice to her?" Mary Plunkett demanded. "I did tell you to be nice to her, didn't I?"

Bernie slammed the door shut behind her. "Of course I was bloody nice to her. I didn't even comment on her stupid botoxed fish lips."

There was a slight pause on the other end. "Good. So she's signed up then?"

"Aye. She reckons he's not cheating on her. So we'll probably find him in bed with her sister or something."

"Kaylie doesn't have a sister," Mary replied primly.

"How do you know her again?" The designer outfit wearing, new car driving Kaylie didn't seem a natural friend for nerdy little Mary Plunkett.

"We met at the gym."

"Sorry, the what?"

Mary laughed. "I know, not where you'd expect me to be, right?"

"That's a bloody understatement. I've been trying to get you to go for more than a year. What was it, a spin class? Don't tell me you're doing weights."

"Um, not exactly. They were doing a free family trial day. A one-hour session for the kids in the creche while the parent worked in the gym. I mean, I'm not going to turn down free childcare, am I?"

"And what exactly did you do in this one hour?"

"I walked on the treadmill. And watched an episode of the new Star Trek series on the wee screen. It was quite nice, actually."

"And will you be going back?"

"God no. I got a blister from my trainers and nearly put my back out when I tripped over a dumbbell. And then Johnny escaped the creche and got into the cupboard with the giant pilates balls. You can imagine how that went."

As usual, Bernie's conversation with Mary was drifting away from the subject at hand.

"How did you meet Kaylie?"

"She works in reception. She helped me get all the pilates balls back up the spiral staircase, which is trickier than you might imagine. Anyway, Kaylie seemed a bit upset, kept checking her phone, that sort of thing, and then when I asked her what was wrong she told me all about it. I mentioned the WWC and there you are."

"And she's convinced there's some reason for her ex to break off the wedding, other than him seeing someone else."

"Yeah."

There was a moment of silence while they both considered the idea.

"I suppose it doesn't have to be another woman," Mary said slowly. "Maybe he's dying of cancer. Or he's gay. Yeah, he's probably gay."

"It's 2024, wouldn't he have just come out already?"

"You never know," Mary replied. "Not every family makes it easy to come out, even nowadays."

"Well if he is gay then the wedding's definitely off," Bernie said. "Either way we have to find out what's going on with the lad. Can you make a start on the research today?"

"I'll do what I can. Remember I'm off to the convention tomorrow."

Bernie grinned. "Ah yes, your little cult gathering."

"It's not a… Never mind. I'm looking forward to it. Walker's working, the kids are at their dads and I'm going to enjoy a little me time."

"While dressed up as a robot toaster or something?"

"Goodbye Bernie." Mary's tone was icy.

"Bye."

Chapter 2: Liz

A small human was dancing to Crazy Frog while another tiny person balanced a rubber brick on her head. It was five minutes before the nursery was due to open and the kids were loving it. Liz Okoro was not.

She watched as her own child navigated the others with ease, ignoring the boy who was scraping smiley faces into the bricks with a stone and the miniature blond girl who was twerking in a tutu. Since there was more than a decade between her two children, Liz had forgotten just how tense and confusing the nursery playground was. And that was just navigating the parents.

Her phone buzzing was a welcome interruption.

"You free to talk?" Bernie barked.

"For two minutes," Liz said. "I'm dropping Isioma. It's her first week at the school nursery, remember?"

"Oh aye, how's it going."

She glanced over at her daughter who was currently pulling worms out of a plant pot while they waited for the session to start.

"Great."

"I wanted to let you know that I've taken that case. Kaylie might be an idiot, but she's spending her dad's money so it should pay the bills for this month."

Liz made encouraging noises. While she knew the WWC had been going through some lean times recently, it was hard to muster too much enthusiasm for what would no doubt turn out to be yet another cheating spouse case. She much preferred the sort of corporate espionage stuff they had done in the last couple of months, but no one seemed to want that right now. All the bank managers were probably still on their summer holidays in the Algarve.

"I'm going to speak to the boyfriend tomorrow," Bernie continued. "If you could make a start on the social media research for Kaylie and her ex-fiance that would give us a head start."

"Will do."

"Oh, and there's one more thing. You're at Little Helpers' nursery on St George Place, right?"

"Right."

"Kaylie's sister uses the same one. She's got two kids and it's all over her social media. Might be worth striking up a conversation."

Liz grimaced. "I suppose I could. Do you have a picture of her?"

"Sending it through now," Bernie said, then she ended the call.

Back to reality, Liz thought as she put her phone back in her bag and waited for Bernie to send her the file. Liz didn't often feel inadequate. In fact, she had always prided herself on being content in her own skin. But the parents at Invergryff's newest and poshest nursery were making her question her usual implacable self-possession.

"Have you started gymnastics with the wee one yet?" A father with a man-bun and a flannel shirt asked her, shuffling over from where he had been standing.

"Oh, no, not yet." She looked at little Isioma who was currently hanging upside down from a railing in the nursery garden. "She seems flexible enough."

"Sure." The man said, with a fake smile that hinted at disappointment. "We've got Naomi in on the Sunday sessions. It's so important for their coordination."

Naomi seemed to be using that coordination to remove her knickers and go for a wee in the plastic paddling pool.

"You might want to, um…" Liz pointed over to the child and was relieved when the man hurried off to protect his daughter's modesty.

She stood at the side of the playground, waiting for the nursery to open and pretended not to mind that no one else was speaking to her. Thankfully, at that moment her phone buzzed with an email from Bernie. Unfortunately the photographs of Kaylie's sister, one Linda Novak, beautician, were so filtered that apart from her being white while dyed blond hair, there wasn't much Liz would be able to recognise about her.

She looked around the playground but couldn't see anyone

who resembled the picture. Liz tried not to mind that all the other women had formed little groups and were chatting to each other. She had never been brilliant at making mum-friends. When she had had her first son, Sean, it had been a crucial point in her accountancy career. She had returned from maternity leave early, leaving no time for baby groups or toddler sing-a-longs. This time around with Isioma she had decided things would be different. She would be the uber-mum, baking muffins and taking Isioma to all the classes and whatever else people did when they weren't parenting while working sixty-hour weeks.

She had even taken up her own mother's suggestion of cloth nappies, just like they had in the sixties. Well, the cloth nappies had lasted a week and the mother and baby groups hadn't gone much better. The muffins came out of a packet but Isioma never seemed to complain.

And now the new nursery had opened. Dave had persuaded her to send Isioma there for two days a week so that she could focus on her work for the WWC. Which was great, obviously. But the nursery was in the very poshest part of Invergryff with clientele to match. Liz was comfortably well-off, but her mother had been a cleaner and Liz still had a working-class soul. The fancy cars and designer clothing on display at drop-offs had made her feel unsettled. Like she was about to star in a reality show about divorces. The cliques of parents who knew each other had at first seemed intimidating, but now she just found them rather boring. At least Liz spent her days solving murders rather than shopping for shoes. Well, most days anyway.

Eventually, the staff members opened the door to the classroom and Isioma toddled in after her friends quite happily. Liz wouldn't have wanted her daughter to be upset or anything, but perhaps a solitary tear or a plea of 'mum' before she went in would have been nice. Still, Liz thought as she walked back across the carpark, at least she could drive home without having to listen to Baby Shark through the car's stereo system.

As Liz was pondering this state of affairs, she saw a curious thing happen. A black car pulled into a disabled spot outside the nursery and a skinny woman wearing leggings and an oversized hoodie jumped out. She pulled a small female child from the back of the car and hurried up the path to the nursery. Clearly running late, the woman hurried into the building, dragging the girl behind her.

Just at that moment, another car pulled in right in front of the black one. There was plenty of space to park, but this new car, a pristine white SUV, pulled up so close that it seemed to be touching the bumper. This meant that there was no way that the woman from the black car would be able to get out of the parking space.

A woman got out. She was around Liz's age, with long blond extensions that didn't make her look any younger. Her face was pinched tight with tension. This woman had an older child who scurried off in the direction of the school once the car door was opened. A second child was taken into the playground and the woman stood next to Liz while the nursery teacher took him inside.

"Nice car," Liz said, desperate to work out what had just happened.

The woman noticed her stare and offered Liz a wide grin.

"It'll teach the killer bitch a lesson," she said, then she turned and walked away along the pavement.

Liz's eyes widened. At that moment she realised two things. Firstly, the woman was wearing the same coat as one of the pictures of Linda Novak, so it was likely that this was the unfiltered version. And the second thing was that the new nursery was turning out to be much more interesting than she had first thought.

Chapter 3: Walker

Sargeant Owen Walker had been working shifts for long enough that he only let out a slight groan when he had to get out of bed at six o'clock on Saturday morning. It added to his feeling of early morning disorientation that he was in his own flat, for once. Ninety per cent of the time now he stayed over at Mary's place, and the kids had even stopped rolling their eyes when he came downstairs in his pyjamas in the morning. But no one wants to wake up four kids any earlier than necessary, so they had both agreed that when he was on an early shift he would make himself scarce.

He didn't enjoy it, though. Brushing his teeth in silence should have been a treat, but he found himself missing the sounds of Supernatural streaming from Mary's telly. While making his bowl of cereal he found himself grinning at the memory of the time Johnny swapped the sugar bowl with salt, and the ensuing fall-out. He had gone from someone with very little interest in children to a pseudo-step-dad-type-figure. Or a fun-uncle, depending on how you looked at it. Vikki had insisted on calling him 'mum's boo' for a while, which he hadn't loved, but it was better than the time that Peter had been studying medieval history and referred to him as the 'swain'.

Eager to leave the eerie silence of his place, he headed into the office early.

"You're keen," his partner, Sergeant Rav Sangar, said when they met at the coffee machine.

"You're keener," Walker smiled, "what time did you get here?"

"Half an hour ago," Rav admitted. "My wee brother, Deep, he got in from the pub at three. Decided to make himself a toastie and set the fire alarm off."

Walker grimaced. "Let me guess, your mum was not impressed." Rav had already told him that his mother ruled the house with an iron fist.

"I don't reckon Deep will be allowed out for a year," Rav chuckled. "Or longer. Probably until he gets married. She's absolutely raging."

"I don't know how you manage to stay living at home," Walker said. "I moved out when I was eighteen and never went back."

Rav took a gulp of his coffee. "It's the culture, isn't it. Besides, have you seen the price of houses these days? We're just poor immigrants remember?"

"Aye," Walker laughed, "Sure, but didn't you tell me your parents own eight shops and about half of the flats in Invergryff?"

"Nah, that doesn't sound right," Rav winked at him. "Just as long as you're buying lunch today. Fancy that new pizza place?"

"I think we're heading off to Glasgow today, aren't we?"

"Oh, that's right I forgot, with your pal Macleod. It'll be good to be out of the office for a while."

Walker nodded. Most of the last few months had been spent either at Tulliallan at the police college, or at the station, completing training exercises. With just a few days left until they would find out if they had passed the final exam, things were becoming tense. Walker would be glad to get some air.

"You're not still worrying about your detective's exam are you?" Rav asked after a few moments of silence.

Walker shrugged. "No... I mean, there's nothing I can do about it now."

"You're one of the smartest cops I've worked with. I bet you'll be fine."

"Thanks. Only book smarts and street smarts are two different things," Walker said, running a hand over his chin. "And I reckon only one of them applies to me."

"Enough feeling sorry for yourself," Rav replied, wagging his index finger in Walker's face. "I'm sure you smashed it."

It was just like at school, Walker thought. None of his clever friends who breezed through their exams ever imagined it was possible that Walker could fail. He worked hard, he didn't skive off or take the Mickey out of the teacher, so it had to be easy to pass, right? Wrong, as his grades showed. It wasn't until his girlfriend had helped him understand what was wrong with him, had told him the word 'dyslexic', that Walker had begun to understand that he hadn't just been a stupid kid.

Having to do an exam that was vital not just to his work, but to the rest of his life, hadn't been a glorious experience. He had just about managed to put some vaguely acceptable answers down, but he knew he'd be lucky to get the pass mark.

Walker shook his shoulders to get rid of the memory.

"Anyway, tell me what we're doing today."

The other officer took the hint and changed the subject. "Macleod's due in a couple of hours. We're to complete some training modules before then."

Walker managed to stifle a groan as they headed back to their desks to work on their paperwork. He put on his headphones and tried to concentrate on the endless flow of words that spread down the screen. His screen reader program helped, but the words still danced in front of his eyes if he didn't take regular breaks. He was glad to see DI Macleod enter the room just as he was starting to lose the will to live.

"I heard you've been assigned to me today," Macleod said, slapping a hand on Walker's shoulder.

"That's right," Walker said, returning the smile. The man from the islands was looking well, Walker was pleased to see. After a recent health scare and a diabetes diagnosis, Macleod – or rather Mrs Macleod – had started a new healthy eating and fitness regime. The DI might complain about it, but his waistline had shrunk and his face had regained its ruddy colour.

Rav walked over and shook hands with Macleod who led them out to the carpark.

Walker climbed into the back with Macleod in the passenger seat and Rav driving. While they pulled out of the station,

Macleod turned on his tablet and started to give them a quick briefing.

"We're off to the conference centre in Glasgow today," Macleod told them. "For something that might be a bit of nothing, but it's just about interesting enough to warrant a visit from SCD."

Intrigued, Walker leaned forward so that he could hear them over the sound of the traffic.

"The reason you two are with me today is we're looking at possible hate speech. Now, I don't have to tell you that it's a bit of a buzzword in the force at the moment. Half the calls to the non-emergency police number are about something our Sandra said about our Noreen on social media. But every so often there is something worthy of a full investigation. And it's good for you to see how to handle these things."

Macleod took a sip of water from his insulated bottle. "So this is where we are today. We've had a report of some death threats concerning a minor celebrity. And not just the usual 'you should hang yourself' online stuff. Actual letters. So we want to take this one seriously."

Something was tickling the back of Walker's mind. "Did you say it was at an event in Glasgow?"

"That's right, some big get-together for TV fans or something."

"It's the con, right?"

Just as he realised that DI Macleod was going to ask something like 'who's conning who?', Walker held up his hand.

"It's short for convention. There's a sci-fi convention in Glasgow this weekend. I know because Mary's going."

"With the kids?"

"No."

"Then she might be able to help us out." Macleod tapped the file on the screen. "I don't have a clue about any of this celebrity stuff. The only thing I watch on the telly is the Six Nations."

"Who's involved in the case?" Rav asked.

"There's been a series of threats issued to the members of a television production called… for God's sake, is this really a thing? It says here it's called *Vampyra: Dragon Rider*?"

Walker laughed. "*Vampyra*? Wow, 'for dragons or death' indeed!"

Even Rav craned his head around from the driver's seat to stare.

Walker swallowed. "Ah, sort of an in-joke. That show has vampires riding dragons and that's what they shout before they go off to war. The dragons that is."

"Thank you for enlightening us," Macleod said, his island lilt turning icy. "I don't think it really matters what sort of show it is. Only that someone has taken to threatening the actors. And it only started a couple of days ago when they arrived in

Glasgow. The letters were hand-delivered, which means we're not dealing with some creep halfway around the world. It's a local."

The car went quiet while that sunk in.

"What did the threats say?"

"I'll let you both read the file before we go in, but basically your standard 'do what I say or die'. Apparently the author of the notes was angry at some plot point in the last series. Maybe Walker can enlighten us?"

"Um, I've only seen series one. Mary's the expert."

"Then we'll need to speak to her soon. I don't suppose she's at the convention?"

"You think she'd miss out on something like that? It's the first time there's been an SFF convention of this size in Glasgow for twenty years."

That earned him another eye-roll from the DI.

"Our job is to de-escalate the situation. Discover who is writing the threats and make sure they don't have an opportunity to follow through on them. And do it all while navigating the new hate crime laws so that we make sure we're doing everything by the book."

"Sounds easy," Rav said with a grin. "Celebrities, politics and crime. What could possibly go wrong?"

Neither Macleod nor Walker felt like answering that one.

Chapter 4: Mary

Mary Plunkett wasn't normally an early riser, but on this Saturday morning she made sure that she was up a full hour before the kids. Matt was picking them up first thing so that she would have time to go to Glasgow for the start of the con. Despite what Bernie might think, Mary was not planning on dressing up. Not in costume anyway. But she had bought some special items to wear for the day.

It was like signalling which tribe you belonged to, Mary thought as she pulled on a t-shirt with an illustration of the most recent Doctor Who pointing a sonic screwdriver at the brothers from Supernatural. From experience she knew that the con would have the anime geeks, the elf-loving fantasy crowd, the computer game nerds and of course every telly fandom you could think of. Mary was very much of the nineties geeky telly nostalgia tribe. And she couldn't wait to meet her fellow tribe members.

She took out her prize possession. It hadn't even made it out of the tissue paper so far. The over-sized hoodie was a slightly unfortunate shade of lurid green, but to those in the know, even the colour would signal the TV show she was currently obsessed with. *Vampyra: Dragon Rider* was described as '*Game of Thrones* meets *Twilight*', but for Mary it was just an excellent example of good clean mindless fun. It had started off as an anime show, then made the crossover to a TV show filmed in the Scottish Highlands. The setting and the use of several Scottish actors had made it a cult hit, especially with the locals.

Mary pulled the hoodie over her head and looked at herself with satisfaction in the mirror. Over her chest was the main character, Vampyra, with her dragon mate Aurolos coiled around the shoulder and onto the back of the garment. It had cost more than it should have to get the hoodie shipped over from Japan, but then Mary barely ever spent money on herself. So far all her earnings from the WWC had been needed to keep her kids in chicken nuggets and school shoes. But now that she was a partner in the business, she had a little spending cash. The hoodie and the convention tickets had been the most she had spent on herself in years, but she was determined not to feel guilty about it. As a single mum, having her own interests was as essential for her well-being as her evening meditations and daily iron pills.

"Why can't we come?" A pouting face announced from the bedroom door.

"It's more of a mum thing," Mary told her. "And I think you kids might still be banned after that thing that Peter said to the Stormtrooper last time we went to a comicon."

"Ugh, boys ruin everything."

Mary wondered if she should correct her, but decided her daughter wasn't exactly wrong. "Look, I'm sure you're going to have much more fun camping than hanging around in a big crowd of people fighting over trading cards."

"You always said camping was the unholy trinity of mud, sleepless nights and midges."

"Did I?" Mary said, feeling vaguely worried. It did sound like something she would say. "Still, you like all that nature stuff. And besides, Daddy and Stephanie are taking you to Loch Lomond. You're going to do canoeing!"

"Can I tip my brothers out of the canoe into the loch?"

"No. But you can splash stinky loch water into their faces."

"Excellent." The face disappeared back upstairs.

A flurry of backpacks, spare socks and a hunt for wellies later all the kids were ready and waiting on the sofa for their father. Mary managed to keep them busy by singing songs and playing silly word games until Matt's car turned up in the drive. Stephanie was in the passenger seat, but Mary was glad to see that she didn't get out of the car. Matt's new partner was perfectly nice and Mary had made an effort to get along with her. But that didn't mean that it wasn't tiring being so chirpy to the woman who got to spend so much time with Mary's own children.

"Miss you mum," Lauren said as the others rushed past to climb into the car. Mary gave her another quick hug and breathed in her little girl hair smell. Then she made sure to release her daughter quickly and wave as she got to the car. It might break Mary's heart, but she knew it was for the best.

"What the hell are you wearing?" Matt said as he took the suitcase from Mary's hand. He was wearing clothes that would have suited a man a decade younger and a couple of stone lighter, but Mary didn't feel the need to say so.

She looked down at her hoodie and felt a flush of shame that she hadn't experienced since her divorce. "It's for one of the shows at the con. The actors are all going to be there. It's going to be fun," she finished, her voice artificially chirpy.

"You never went to anything like that when we were married," Matt commented.

Mary had to stifle a laugh. "Yeah, funny that. Maybe I thought you wouldn't be completely one-hundred-per-cent supportive?"

"You mean I would have laughed and called you a nerd? You're probably right."

She didn't argue with the point. In fact, Mary would never have even bothered to ask. The snide look at the question would have been enough to break her spirit. She thought back to Walker's only comment when she had texted him about the con.

Can you get me Spiderman's autograph?

Matt climbed into the car and Mary waved the kids off with a smile. She noted with a little satisfaction Stephanie's expression when Peter showed her his latest obsession: a stick insect called Gary who went everywhere in a mason jar.

"Have fun," Mary called out, giving them a final wave, then closing the front door firmly behind her.

Chapter 5: Bernie

Ryan Porter lived in one of the housing estates in the eastern suburbs of Invergryff. The house had been extended over the years and someone had converted the garage. Bernie noted that they had also followed the modern trend of razing all plants to the ground and replacing them with astroturf.

Bernie checked her notes as she sat in the car. Ryan lived here with his mother, his dad having died not long ago. He had been going out with Kaylie for two years, up until the recent dumping.

She rang the doorbell and was glad to see a young man answer the door. Bernie knew it was better to leave the mother until she had spoken to the source of all the drama himself.

"Can I help you?" He wore the standard uniform of a mid-twenties lad: joggies that hung a bit too low on his hips and an oversized t-shirt that proclaimed he was a supporter of the local football team. Strike one against him, Bernie thought. She despised football, particularly the sort of men who watched it avidly but couldn't run from one end of the pitch to the other.

"Ryan Porter?"

He nodded confirmation.

"Can I have a wee word? I'm a friend of Kaylie's."

"Really?" The man didn't look convinced. "You're a bit more... mature than most of her friends."

"We met at the UTI clinic," Bernie said, knowing that would prevent further questions. It did.

The lad scratched the back of his ear. "Well, it was nice to meet you, but Kaylie and I... Well, we're not exactly –"

"You dumped her."

A red blush spread up from the man's neck. "We broke up last week. So if you're looking for her, you'd be best going over to her place."

He shifted position just enough that Bernie managed to get a foot in the doorway.

"Actually it's yourself I'd like to speak to. How about you make me a black coffee? I'd prefer filtered but I'll take instant if you've nothing else."

Bernie often found that when faced with rudeness, people capitulated. Ryan Porter was no different. His jaw worked for a few seconds, then he nodded.

"All right. Kitchen's in the back."

She was already making her way there. Clearly the mother wasn't in. From what Kaylie had told her, there was no way that Ryan Porter's mother wouldn't have come in to see what all the fuss was about.

The kitchen was clean but small, and Porter had to shuffle past the table to put the kettle on. A large jar of instant was produced, but Bernie decided not to complain. Porter was already going to find the conversation difficult enough.

"I don't really understand what you're after," the man asked once he had handed over the mug of coffee. "I mean, it's just like I said. Kaylie and I aren't together anymore."

"And why would that be?"

"I don't see that that's any of your business."

Bernie snorted a laugh. "Come on lad, you should have thought of that before you let me in and made me a cuppa."

Ryan stared up at the ceiling as if he thought that by ignoring Bernie then he wouldn't have to deal with her. No such luck.

"Kaylie is very upset."

"I know. I never meant to hurt her."

What an annoying phrase, Bernie thought to herself. And a nice way of getting out of saying sorry. "You did. She bought a bloody wedding dress, did you know that? So I reckon you owe the poor lass an explanation."

Ryan rubbed the heel of his hand into his eyes. "I just can't get married right now. It wouldn't be fair to Kaylie. There's a lot going on at home. My mum... well, it's not the right time."

Bernie rolled her eyes. She couldn't stand mummy's boys. One of the things that had attracted her to Finn was that his mother was long dead.

"Look, I've got a free weights class in twenty-five minutes, I'd rather not waste my time. Let's face it. If you hadn't been such a coward and told Kaylie the truth, then I wouldn't have needed to come at all. Now you tell me the whole story, and I'll decide how much of it Kaylie needs to know."

Like all weak men, Ryan actually looked relieved that someone else was taking over the conversation.

"I guess I could tell you some of it. Then maybe Kaylie might not think I'm a total asshole after all. You know she threw my clothes out in the street."

"Good for her," Bernie nodded in satisfaction. "Now start talking."

Ryan let out a sigh. "It started at Christmas. You see, my sister got her one of those DNA kits. Some place on the High Street had a special offer on them. Buy one get one free. You know?"

"I'm familiar with the concept."

He blinked. "Anyhow, my sister thought it would be a laugh. She did one ages ago, god knows why. She's into all that family history crap. Thinks she's related to some old King or something."

"Can we focus on what happened with your mum?"

"Oh yeah. So me and mum did the tests. And mum said wouldn't it be easier to just get all the results sent to her place."

"Right," Bernie said, her detective senses already kicking in.

"Did she say why?"

"No. And I never thought about it. Why would I? And then the results came back, and they were just the same as my sisters. So that was that."

"Only it wasn't?"

He shook his head. "I don't even know why I did it. Mum had told me the results over the phone, but when I asked to see the letter, she said she couldn't remember where she put it. And then I was around at her house one day when she was out in the garden. And I found it."

"And it showed you something you weren't expecting?"

"It said that I was half Irish – that's my mum's background – but half Eastern European. Now, my dad was as Scottish as you like. Fourth generation Greenock. So where the hell did the Eastern European bit come from?"

"I guess your mum can answer that one."

He sniffed. "I went straight over to her and she just burst into tears. Apparently she'd had a 'bit of a fling' around then with an HGV driver. My dad never even got his license."

"Must have been a shock," Bernie said as the man rubbed at his eyes. "Still, not something to worry about. Happens all the time. Right?"

His narrowed eyes suggested that had been the wrong thing to say.

"I loved my dad," Ryan continued, his voice wobbling. "Before he died we'd go to the football every week, with my granddad and all. Three generations of Invergryff Town supporters, we used to say. Now what if I'm... what? A Sparta Prague supporter?"

"I can see you've got to the heart of the issue," Bernie replied. "But now look. Surely none of this is worth breaking up your relationship for?"

"How can I get married without even knowing my dad's name?"

"Your mum didn't tell you it?"

"She said it was Marty something. That she couldn't remember now. I might have got a bit annoyed at that. Called her a few names. And now she's not speaking to me either."

The sobs started now in earnest. Bernie stared at the ceiling, wondering how long it would take the man to get a hold of himself. She was getting a crick in her neck from all the sympathetic head-tilting.

"What if I could look into it for you," she said, after the wailing showed no sign of stopping. "I have a bit of a knack for that sort of thing. Maybe I could try and get his name for you at least. Then you could get married and Kaylie won't have to throw that dress in the bin."

"Would you?" Ryan looked up at her with bloodshot eyes. "That would be amazing."

"Yeah," Bernie grinned at her own moment of altruism. "I'll

even give you a half-price discount on my usual rates."

"Oh."

Five minutes later, Bernie had a new client on the books. She returned to her car and sat back in the driver's seat feeling satisfied. Find the enigmatic Marty, convince the idiot Ryan to put the wedding back on and that would be two cases wrapped up in a nice bow.

Simple.

Chapter 6: Liz

Liz got home from dropping Isioma at her grandmother's house and made sure that Dave wasn't home before she put the telly on to catch up with the latest episode of Wet Dreamz. It was the sort of show she used to slag other people off for watching. Ten men and ten women had to go on a date every week. So far so much like every other dating show. The USP of this show was that they had to do it in a swimming pool, with the women in barely-there bikinis and the men in speedos that left far too little to the imagination. Liz had happened upon the first episode, started watching ironically and was now obsessed. Last week they had actually had a foam party. And one of the lads had 'lost' his trunks live on telly, giving him his thirty seconds of fame and a million new social media followers.

She had just settled down with a coffee and a fluffy cushion to lounge against when the doorbell rang. With a sigh, Liz powered off the telly and made her way to the front door, where someone was already letting themselves in.

"Only me," Bernie said as she shut the door behind her.

"It's generally considered polite to wait to be let in," Liz said to her friend.

"Is it? Put the kettle on, will you. I've been talking for an hour and I'm gasping for a coffee."

Liz led them through to the kitchen and did as she was told.

"No laptop out?" Bernie said. "You've normally started work by now."

"Give us a chance. I was just catching up on my messages," Liz replied, glad that she had turned off the telly. She didn't want to hear Bernie's views on her choice of TV show. Considering what Bernie thought about Mary's harmless sci-fi telly, Liz suspected she might be in for some judgment if she revealed her obsession with Dreamz.

"You didn't forget we were having a meeting this morning?" Bernie's eyes narrowed.

"No," Liz lied. "Where's Mary?"

"At her loser's convention," Bernie said promptly.

"I think it's sweet," Liz said, giving her friend a sharp look. "And I don't think Mary's a loser just for doing something she loves."

Bernie ignored this point and brought out her own laptop. "Let's keep focussed on what pays the bills, shall we?"

Resigned, Liz poured herself a large coffee from the hissing silver machine and did the same for her friend.

"Go on then, tell me what's got your bee in a bonnet this early on a Saturday."

"I've been looking into this Kaylie-Ann Michelson case and I'm not too happy about it."

"I know what you mean," Liz agreed. "I can't decide if Kaylie's desperate to be chasing this guy that dumped her or if it shows a bit of backbone. You know, refusing to take no for an answer."

Bernie sniffed. "I already told her to just give up the lad. Trust me, there's nothing special about him. But the woman is determined, I'll give her that. She wants her big white wedding."

"Right. And she probably feels embarrassed. Humiliated even. It'll be all around Invergryff that she got dumped just before the wedding."

"At the end of the day, all that matters is she's willing to pay us to investigate. And that's why I spent this morning at Ryan Porter's place. Turns out the lad's having an identity crisis."

Bernie filled Liz in about Porter not knowing who his father was.

"Sure, there's plenty of people in Invergryff don't know their dads," Liz pointed out once her friend had finished recounting the interview. "If we needed certainty on that point before the wedding then no one here would ever get married."

"I know, but that's what Ryan says is the problem. As stupid as it might seem to us, he won't get married until he knows who his dad is."

Liz tried to appreciate the young man's point of view. It must be a bit of a shock to find out that your dad isn't who you thought he was. But she still didn't see why it would cause you to call off your own wedding.

"Have you told Kaylie this?" she asked.

"Not yet. I was hoping Mary might do it. You know how she's good at the people stuff."

"True," Liz agreed. Mary was one of those people that instantly put strangers at ease. She was the anti-Bernie in that regard.

"And now she's swanned off to this stupid thing in Glasgow just when I need her."

Even for Bernie, this was quite unfair.

"Is that why you're mad?" Liz asked her. "Because Mary's missing one meeting?"

Bernie shrugged. "It's a commitment issue, right? Is it so wrong that I think the WWC should take precedence over her hobbies?"

"And what if I scheduled the next meeting for Sunday morning?" Liz said, knowing that she was poking the bear.

"I have my Alpine walking on Sundays."

"Exactly," Liz said, folding her arms and giving her friend a significant look.

"Tell you what," Bernie sniffed. "If Mary burns off five hundred calories and has abs of steel like I do when she comes back, I'll never mention it again."

Liz sighed. "You genuinely can't see anyone else's point of view, can you?"

"Why should I? It would make life a hell of a lot more difficult."

Impossible, Liz thought. It was truly impossible to win an argument with Bernadette Paterson.

"I'll speak to Kaylie if you want," she said finally, in an attempt to keep the peace.

"Excellent," Bernie grinned.

"Now that's sorted, I can tell you about something weird that happened at the nursery yesterday with Kaylie's sister," Liz said.

"If it's about kids pushing each other or calling each other names you might be better with Mary's advice," Bernie admitted. "I was never much good at any of that. My Ewan basically raised himself once he was potty trained."

"Oh, I think you'll like this one. Someone was accused of being a killer."

A wide, toothy smile filled her friend's face.

"Now that's much more my style."

Chapter 7: Walker

The woman sitting opposite Sergeant Walker was the most beautiful he had ever seen. This was no disrespect to Mary Plunkett, his girlfriend and the most wonderful person he had ever had the good fortune to meet. It was an objective fact. Dark, almost black hair that ran to her shoulders, perfectly formed eyebrows, a hint of blush on the sharp cheekbones. Yes, Anetta Strong was beautiful. But not, Walker was starting to suspect, the sharpest knife in the drawer.

"Normally I get Penelope to deal with all the social media stuff," Anetta explained to the police officers. "I hate seeing all the negativity. And one time I told some guy to get lost when he dissed my acting. After that, the production company told me to get off social media. Good riddance to it, I say. Like, I still do my adverts and stuff, I just run it all through someone else. Haters gonna hate, right?"

Walker was finding her quite hard to follow and he could sense his superior felt the same.

"If we could just focus on the more recent threats," the DI told her. "The ones that came in the post."

She smiled and Walker was reminded of her character on the show. Vampyra only smiled when smiting her enemies, of course, so it was odd to see the woman so relaxed.

"I didn't even know you could get post at a hotel, did you? So when the receptionist handed me the letter, I was totally confused."

"And you were shocked by what was inside?"

A shrug. "I guess so. I mean, it's just like what I used to see all the time on social media 'die bitch die', that sort of thing. It was a bit weird to see it on paper."

Walker looked down at the photocopy in his hands. *You won't make it through another summer. Watch your back.* It was printed by a standard inkjet printer on standard paper. No clues there.

"Are we finished yet?" Anetta flicked her long hair off her shoulder. "I need to speak on one of those tedious panel things and then sign about a million autographs. And there's, like, a serious lack of deodorant in this place, if you get my drift."

"I do think you should be taking this a little more seriously, Ms Strong." Macleod said. "Unfortunately, while it is common to see these sorts of threats online, it is more unusual to receive a physical letter. That's why we have launched an investigation. That, and the fact that you are not the only person to receive a threat."

"Oh, someone said that they sent a letter to Stefan too. I just thought he was making it up. I mean, why would anyone want *him* dead."

"Why would anyone want *you* dead," Walker prompted her in the same tone.

"Oh." She blinked those big fake lashes again. "I guess because I'm the star of the show. And you know, a pretty face, that sort of thing." She giggled. "We know that men hate beautiful women, don't we."

"Some men, perhaps," Macleod said.

Was the Detective Inspector going red in the cheeks? Walker hoped that his superior wasn't going to get all flustered by a self-confessed beautiful woman. The Sergeant was glad that he was past all that, as long as he kept his eyes firmly on the woman's face, he didn't even feel a flicker of attraction. Probably.

Macleod cleared his throat. "With two members of the cast being targeted, particularly at such a public event, we want to ensure that there is a police presence while you are at the convention. This is in addition to the security staff here."

The woman let out a sigh. "I hope I'm not going to be followed about everywhere. I do have a social life to maintain, you know."

Macleod slapped Walker on the back. "My Sergeant here, Owen Walker will make sure you're in good hands."

Anetta looked Walker up and down in a way that he himself had been keen to avoid.

"Well, I suppose that might just do," she said, giving him a wink.

He managed a tight nod. Despite what Macleod said, he didn't think it likely that anyone was going to attempt to murder a third-rate TV star. And now he was going to have to spend the next few hours with a very pretty, very flirtatious movie star. A dream for most people, but not for a man firmly committed to Invergryff's quirkiest private investigator.

At that moment, Rav came over, carrying a paper bag.

"Can I have a word, sir?" He said to Macleod. The Inspector motioned them all to a quiet area at the back of the hall.

"What is it?"

"I've just had a chat with Stefan Alderick. He's the other recipient of the letter."

"I hope he's a bit more concerned than Ms Strong," Macleod said as he watched the woman fix her make-up. "I mean, she doesn't seem to be taking it seriously at all."

"I think he is," Rav replied. "He seemed pretty freaked out that someone had been to the hotel."

"It's the same one that Anetta is staying at, right?"

Rav nodded. "It's attached to the conference venue here. We've already asked for CCTV of the Reception and we've got the techies working on it back at the station. There's a camera right on the desk so we're hoping we might be able to get footage of whoever left the letters."

"The receptionist doesn't remember?"

"It was early in the morning just as the postman was delivering the letters from Royal Mail. He leaves them in a sack at the end of reception and it looks like our guy snuck in and left them on top. No one can remember seeing him. Or her for that matter."

Macleod's mouth turned down at the corners. "Let's hope that CCTV comes through then. I don't like that this guy knew how to deliver the letters without being caught. It's showing a bit more foresight than a casual stalker. Did you get anything else from Stefan?"

"Nothing concrete," Rav frowned. "But the guy did seem worried. He said that he's had some really nasty messages online. I've got him to forward them all to Sergeant Aitchison. He's looking to see if we can match any of these online creeps with our in-person letter writer. But I'm not too sure. The stuff that Stefan has been getting through his social media is mainly homophobic stuff. Apparently his character in the show is bisexual, so you can imagine how the right wing trolls feel about that. But there's no suggestion that homophobia is a motive with the letter."

"It said exactly the same as Anetta's right?"

"Yes. *You won't make it through another summer. Watch your back.* We've sent it to forensics, just like the other one. It would be nice to think there's a great big fingerprint on one of them, but – "

"We're not that lucky, right?" Macleod's tone was morose.

"Right."

"I've got a bad feeling about this one lads," the DI took out his phone. "I'm going to see if the station can spare us any more officers. Maybe if we've got a big enough visual presence then it might scare our guy away."

"You think he's here?" Walker asked, trying not feel the shiver that trickled up his back.

"I'm hoping he's at home in his bedsit watching his show and thinking about all the mischief he's caused. But if there's a chance that he actually means to go through with these threats, then I don't want it to happen on our shift. Rav, you go back to Stefan and keep him in your sights. Walker, you do the same with Anetta. Anything unusual, anyone creeping around that you don't like the look of, call it in straightaway."

"Got it."

The DI pointed at the bag at Rav's chest. "I guess that's some sort of healthy snack, is it?"

"Um, a pack of five doughnuts actually," the man blushed. "I didn't have breakfast."

"Well don't eat them anywhere near me. My wife made me baked oats today and they taste like feet. Enjoy your youth while you can."

The DI stomped away, pressing the phone to his ear.

"I don't think he likes me much," Rav said as they watched him go.

"He's just jealous of your pancreas," Walker replied.

"What?"

"He's diabetic, remember? Maybe lay off the doughnuts next

time."

"Noted," Rav said. "Want one?"

"All right," he said, reaching his hand into the bag and pulling out a sugar-coated piece of loveliness. "I'll need it to keep me going. I get the feeling it's going to be a long day."

Chapter 8: Mary

Mary Plunkett was living her best life. She had picked up the official convention drink – something bright pink, sugary and perfume-smelling – and had a sparkly green lanyard that proclaimed her as one of the fan community. She had already bought four books and a set of stickers featuring Vampyra and her dragon family. And she might have bought personalised Lord of the Rings mini figurines for each of her children for a ridiculous price, but you couldn't turn off being a mum, even for a few hours.

Four people had already told her they loved her hoodie and one person had actually asked for a selfie with her. Mary couldn't keep the smile from her face as she weaved her way around the busy stalls. Surely it didn't get better than this.

"Hello gorgeous," a male voice said beside her.

She spun around to see Walker, grinning at her.

"What are you doing here," she said as she pulled him in for a kiss.

"Oi, no snogging on duty," he said, although it didn't stop him pressing their lips together for a second time. "Do you have time to grab a cuppa?"

"Of course."

They found a spot behind a costume stall that seemed to

specialise in Doctor Who scarves. Mary had already made a note of a couple to purchase later by the time Walker came back with a couple of takeaway cups of tea.

"Someone over there asked if I was cosplaying 'the man'," Walker announced as he sat down next to her.

Mary laughed. "You do look a bit out of place in your suit."

"It's not that bad is it?"

Actually, Mary thought he looked pretty damn good in anything, but she wasn't about to say so. "You haven't told me why you're here."

"Work."

She tilted her head. "Is that all you're going to say?"

"Sorry, you know the drill."

"I do, and you know that I'll find out eventually anyway," she said, softening her words with a smile.

"Isn't that the fun bit? Did you buy anything at the stalls?"

"Too much probably, I've spent a bloody fortune."

"Aye, but when did you last spend some money on yourself? And I'm not counting that box of chocolates you bought the other week. You gave all of them to the kids."

"They left me the Turkish delight," she reminded him.

"Which you don't like."

"True."

They sipped their teas in happy silence for a moment.

"You didn't ask about the exam result," Walker said.

Mary bit her lip. "I didn't want to ask. You haven't heard yet then?"

"No."

She squeezed his hand. "Whatever happens, you know that I'm super proud that you did it, right?"

"Right." He gave her a brave smile. "Everyone else is just saying not to worry about it. Easy to say when you're used to passing the bloody things. But I know I gave it my best shot and if not there's always the resits."

"You'll get there," Mary reassured him. "Whether by the quick way or the longer way, you're going to pass."

"Thanks."

Mary finished her drink and popped the cup into the recycling bin. "I'm off to the *Vampyra* panel now. Can't wait."

"Oh yeah?"

Mary noticed him stand a little straighter.

"That's not who you're here for, is it?"

"I told you, I can't say," Walker said. It was lucky he was pretty, Mary thought, because her boyfriend was a dreadful liar.

"Sure. Well, make sure there are no murders, right?"

"Right," Walker said, his mouth a grimace. He glanced down at his watch. "Break's over. Better head off. Don't run off with a Klingon now will you?"

She watched him walk away. The day had just got even more interesting. Why had he looked so pale when she had suggested murder? Was one of her favourite actors really in trouble? Time to head over to the auditorium and find out.

It took her a good fifteen minutes to make her way through the crowd of superheroes and anime characters. Mary finally reached the main room only to see that it was packed full of fans. Extraordinary, considering that a year ago *Vampyra* had been a little-known show on a small network. Then it had been picked up by a larger streaming service and had bloomed into a major show. People like Mary, who had been there since the start, tended to look down on the new fans with a sort of tender, patronizing acceptance.

"There's a couple of seats at the front," a steward with punky blond tipped hair and a nose ring told her. "Two guys got chucked out a minute ago. They had spent a little too long in the convention bar."

Delighted, Mary shuffled into one of the spare chairs, smiling at a gender-neutral elf person who was sitting next to her.

"Team Elrik or Team Puffer," the Elf asked.

"Oh, definitely Team Puffer," Mary replied. "Do you know if either of them are going to be on the panel?"

"Anetta is the only one that's been officially announced," her neighbour explained. "But I'm hoping that Stefan might turn up." Stefan Alderick was the actor who played Elrik. He was extraordinarily handsome with Nordik features and long blond hair. The scruffier Marco Naples who played the adventurer Puffer was much more Mary's type.

She was about to ask her new friend if Marco might be coming when the lights dimmed and the opening music to *Vampyra* began to blare out of the speakers. Mary whooped along with the rest of the audience as three people made their way onto the stage.

Anetta Strong was incredible. She moved like a supermodel, slinking across the stage and holding up her hand to take the applause. She was beautiful like a sculpture or a painting. Mary was dying to know her skin care regime although she had a suspicion that she wouldn't have been able to afford it.

Next to Anetta was a woman that Mary only recognised from the convention programme. Tiana Schmidt was a tiny little thing, pretty with dark hair and bronze skin. She looked a little nervous in front of the crowd, but she got nearly as big a cheer as Anetta. As a make-up artist famous for working on some huge science-fiction and fantasy shows, she was nearly as popular as the actors.

The third man got less of a cheer, as money men often do. His name was Tony Ashley and he was the Executive Producer. Thin to the point of gaunt with a well-manicured goatee, he looked a little out of place in his smart suit in a room full of people in t-shirts and cosplay.

"He's the one that tried to sell out to the big broadcasters," her next-door neighbour whispered to her. "He was planning to get rid of the gay romance just so it would get picked up."

Mary nodded. She had heard that rumour too, but hoped it wasn't true. *Vampyra* had been picked up by a major distributor anyway, even with the gay storyline so maybe Ashley hadn't done what the forums were accusing him of.

A fourth man appeared on the stage and this time Mary didn't know him.

"Who's that?" she whispered to the Elf.

"That's the chair. He's one of the writers. Tim something, I think?"

Mary peered at the man who had a short ginger beard and glasses. *Vampyra* was written by a team of between four and six people depending on the season so the writers didn't tend to get much publicity.

"I think it's Tim Errin," Mary said, dredging up the name from the recesses of her memory. "I read an article by him once."

Errin cleared his throat. "Thank you all for coming today. Can I get another round of applause for our cast and crew of *Vampyra* for coming to talk to us?"

There was a warm response from the crowd.

"The topic of today's panel is: *Vampyra*, the making of a legend. And we're going to focus on that process and how it all came about. But first I want to introduce you to my fellow panellists. On the far right, we have Tony Ashley, our Executive Producer and general boss man, then we have Tiana Schmidt who is responsible for hair and make-up and our wonderful dragon skin creations. And last is someone you're used to seeing on screen, the wonderful Anetta Strong, Vampyra herself."

Of the three, only Anetta stood up at her name, ensuring that her applause continued for longer than anyone else's. The panel began answering questions that Tim Errin asked them. It became clear to Mary quite early on that Errin wasn't a brilliant chair. He was clearly too afraid to interrupt anyone which meant the audience was treated to a ten minute monologue about the future of television by Tony Ashley.

Anetta on the other hand seemed to answer every question as quickly and briefly as she could. If anything, Mary thought she looked a little bored. The only time she came to life was when she was asked where she saw the series going next.

"What we really want is a *Vampyra* movie," Anetta offered them another smile. "Can you imagine how cool that would be?"

This earned her some cheers from the crowd.

"That would be amazing, of course, and you never know what might happen," the producer said, although Mary thought he didn't seem too convinced.

"But I have some other exciting projects coming up that I know you guys will like," Anetta said, leaning forward towards the audience. "I'm going to be appearing in my first theatre show next month and I –"

Gasps from the crowd to the right of the stage gave away that something was happening. Mary looked over to see a tall, rangy figure striding onto the stage.

"It's Elrik," the Elf squealed, forgetting the man's real name in their excitement. "He's here!"

Stefan Alderick aka Elrik Elf-kin strode to the centre of the stage and put up his hands, accepting the growing round of applause.

"Hi guys," he waved and blew a kiss to the crowd.

For a brief moment, a flash of fury passed over Anetta's features. Then she put her hands together and began to clap along with everyone else. Her smile was wide and Mary wondered if she had imagined the previous expression.

But Mary had spent an unfortunate amount of the last two years among dangerous and criminal individuals. And she couldn't shake the sense that Anetta had been absolutely livid. If looks could kill, then Stefan Alderick would already be dead.

Chapter 9: Bernie

It was growing late on Saturday before Bernie had a chance to drive back over to Ryan Porter's house from the gym. It was non-negotiable for her to do some sort of weights session at the weekend, and she certainly wasn't going to let the case of an absent father ruin that.

A quick shower and a protein shake later, she was back in the car calling up Liz on the hands free.

"Did you get a chance to speak to Kaylie yet?" Bernie asked as soon as her friend answered the phone.

"And it's nice to hear from you too," Liz said grumpily. "I can't talk long, Dave's just brought Isioma home and she's high as a kite." The happy sounds of a toddler smashing something valuable could be heard in the background.

"All right, just tell me if you saw Kaylie."

"Not in person yet, but I did call her. I told her what you said about Ryan, but she didn't seem convinced."

"She didn't?"

"No. I think her exact words were: 'who gives a crap about his dad, I've just had to send back two hundred origami swans'."

"Two hundred what?"

"Wedding favours I think. Kaylie said that she didn't care

what his reason was, she needed him to confirm the wedding was still on by the end of the week. They've got to pay the balance on the venue by then."

Bernie rolled her eyes. "And I'm guessing that it's somewhere posh, right?"

"That new country club over by East Kilbride. I reckon it cost her twenty grand at least."

"Cost her dad you mean," Bernie replied. She pulled the car into the drive of a familiar building. "All right, we better get a move on with this case. I'm just outside Ryan Porter's house right now. He's let me know that his mum's just come back from the bingo."

"And you're just going to barge in there and ask about her deepest darkest secret."

"Of course," Bernie shrugged. "What else am I going to do?"

"I just... I mean, maybe it's a moment for a bit of tact. Aren't the client's mothers on your list of people we don't let you talk to?"

"Nope. The recently bereaved, young children and anyone with an anxiety order." Bernie ticked them off on her fingers. "Mothers of cheeky young lads are fair game."

Liz went quiet for a moment. "Fine. I can't think of a reason to stop you. But remember, try not to get her back up before you find out some details of this affair she had. Otherwise, we've got bugger all to go on. Looking for a Polish guy who might not even still be in the country is not going to be easy."

"That's what we get paid the big bucks for," Bernie replied. "Or in this case, the distinctly average bucks."

"Right, well, I'd better let you go then," Liz said. "Remember –"

"Don't get her back up. Yeah, I got it," Bernie said, clicking off the call. She got out of her car and walked up the driveway for her second visit of the day.

When Bernie rang the bell it didn't seem like Mrs Porter was in the mood to answer it. Instead of coming to the door, the woman went to the living room window and peeked out between the curtains.

Bernie gave her a cheery wave. "Going to let me in, hen?"

Reluctantly, Mrs Porter made her way around to the door and opened it a couple of inches. A fake-tanned face with hair that was last in style two decades ago peered out at her.

"Who are you?"

"A private investigator. Didn't Ryan tell you I was coming?"

"He did, and I'm telling you what I told him. Get lost."

Mrs Porter went to slam the door but she hadn't reckoned on Bernie's size seven trainer being in the way.

"Now that's not very nice," Bernie said to her, showing her teeth in something that might have been called a smile if you didn't look at her eyes. "You don't have to let me in, of course. And I'll just stand out here on the doorstep. Maybe I'll make a few calls back to the office about how the woman who lied about her own son's dad won't let me in. And maybe I'll do it in my outside voice."

As Bernie had thought she might, Mrs Porter winced at the volume. "Fine," she said once she realised she was out of options. "You can come in for five minutes. Then you can crawl back under whatever rock you came from."

Most women would feel affronted at this sort of welcome, but it wasn't even the worst thing that anyone had said to Bernie that week. Or that day, for that matter.

"So Ryan sent you, did he? Too scared to talk to my face now, I suppose." Mrs Porter said down on one of the stools in the kitchen. Under the downlighters she looked old and tired, like she was being weighed down by life. Bernie reckoned she needed a bit more iron in her diet, but Mary and Liz had banned her from bringing up nutritional advice during interviews, for some strange reason.

"He wants to know who his dad is," Bernie said simply. "You can understand why the lad's upset."

"He knew exactly who his dad was. The man that raised him. He'll be turning in his grave."

Bernie leaned back against the counter. The kitchen hadn't got any larger since her earlier visit, and Mrs Porter's resentment was making it feel smaller still.

"Now, I've always wondered about that," Bernie said, watching the other woman glare at a spot somewhere out of the window. "Surely one of the few upsides to dying was not having to worry about this sort of thing."

Instead of answering, Mrs Porter took out a disinfectant spray and started scrubbing at the counters.

"Ryan just wants to know who his biological father was before he gets married. Surely that's not too much to ask."

Mrs Porter barked out a single syllable laugh. "That's the only good thing to come out of all this, him postponing the wedding. I never liked that Kaylie girl. All boobs and no brains."

"Ach, if men valued boobs as much as brains it would be a very different world," Bernie told her.

The other woman gave a sharp nod of agreement.

"Was that what Ryan's dad was interested in," Bernie said, tired of the softly softly approach and going for the jugular instead. "Was he more into your boobs than your brains?"

"Jesus, you've no respect have you."

"No. It's one of my better qualities. Look, I can tell you don't want me here. Even I can read these sorts of signals. But the sooner you give me what I want, the sooner you never have to see me again."

A few seconds ticked by. Mrs Porter was doing her best evil eye impression, but those things never bothered Bernie. Eventually, the woman's posture sort of crumpled.

"Fine. Follow me."

Ryan's mum led them through to the living room, somewhere Bernie hadn't seen before. To her dismay, it had been 'interior designed' with a bit too much emphasis on glass and shining metal to be considered homely. The place was so tidy that Bernie wondered if Ryan was even allowed inside. She couldn't imagine the hulking lad would be able to turn around without bumping into something fragile.

Bernie approved of the cleanliness, although the amount of mirrored furniture made her edgy. Every time she moved a hundred half-reflections moved too, making her feel motion sick.

"Don't bother sitting down," Mrs Porter said, just in case Bernie was imagining there was any attempt to be hospitable. "This won't take long."

Bernie tried to find a spot where she was unlikely to be met by a hundred mirror versions of herself and waited while the woman rooted around in a set of drawers.

"Here. I shouldn't even be showing you this, but it's the only photo I've got."

It was a photo probably from the late nineties, back when you had to take your film to the chemists to get it printed out. It was curled at the edges and the people were slightly out of focus. Still, it was just about possible to recognise Ryan's mum as the woman on the sofa. She had a decent figure back then, Bernie thought, with a tight black t-shirt and skinny jeans. The man around her looked slightly older, with a shock of white-blond hair and some sort of band t-shirt with a skull on it.

"This is Marty?"

"That's right. The only picture I've got of him. We weren't exactly going out for long."

Mrs Porter's lips were pressed together, like even saying this much was painful for her.

"Why didn't you just tell Ryan?" Bernie asked. "I mean, it's not like it was the sixties. Plenty of single mothers were around in the nineties."

"I met my husband when Ryan was just a few months old. Marty hadn't even managed to stick around for the birth. So Ryan grew up with Will Porter as his dad. It wasn't that we lied, we just never told him otherwise. He assumed that the man he had known all his life was his real dad, so what would be the point in him knowing otherwise."

"Only now Ryan's found out and he's upset with you."

"It's like living with a teenager again. He storms upstairs to his room and doesn't come out. And now all this stuff about the wedding. It's a bloody mess."

"He wants to find out who his dad is," Bernie reminded her. "Is that so bad?"

"I just don't know what to tell him. Marty said his last name was Gortat, but when he vanished after I told him I was pregnant, it turned out that wasn't his name at all."

"How do you mean?"

Mrs Porter picked an invisible piece of fluff from the sofa. "I went to see if I could find him. He wasn't answering his phone, but I knew the site he worked on. And they just... well, they laughed at me. Said I must be 'one of Marty's girls' and that he'd gone off back to Poland. And they said Gortat wasn't even his real last name. That he'd changed it when he came over here."

"Did you tell Ryan this?"

She shook her head. "I got the feeling... well, from what the men at the building site said, he might have been in trouble with the police. That's why he was always moving on, using different names. And I didn't want Ryan to know that his dad was a criminal."

Mrs Porter's head might have drooped at this new information, but Bernie found it was energising her. If Marty turned out to be a wrong'un then the case might be more interesting than they had first assumed.

"Look, I know you want to just sweep all this under the rug, but the truth is out now," Bernie said. "And at the moment it's a sort of half-truth that will leave Ryan always wanting more information. Let us help you on this. We'll find out who Marty really was and what he's up to now. Then everyone can move on with their lives."

The other woman still didn't look too pleased, but she did manage a small nod.

"You'll see yourself out."

Even Bernie knew that that was her cue to leave. Mrs Porter was still sitting on the sofa, clutching the photo and staring into space, when she shut the door.

Chapter 10: Liz

Liz reckoned that Bernie was still mad at Mary about her going to the convention. This was partly little things: when Mary arrived for the WWC meeting on Saturday night Bernie hadn't offered her a drink or brought out the fancy biscuits. And then there were the less subtle methods that made the woman's feelings clear.

"I still can't believe you missed our earlier meeting for the stupid loser convention," Bernie said as soon as Mary sat down at the table.

"I'm here now, aren't I?" Mary grumbled. "Count yourself lucky. I'm missing a musical version of Edwin A Abbott's cult classic *Flatland*. And there's two dancing dogs in it, not to mention a hexagon playing the piano."

Even Liz found this baffling.

"A waste of time," Bernie repeated. "Especially when we're so busy."

"It didn't feel like a waste of time when I found out about the death threats," Mary replied, meeting Bernie's glare with one of her own.

"Death threats?"

"That's right. Walker was at the con with DI Macleod. Apparently, the cast of *Vampyra* has been receiving some nasty letters. Hand-delivered letters, no less."

"Now that does sound interesting," Bernie replied, shuffling forward in her seat. "What did you manage to find out?"

"Oh, so now you're interested in the loser convention, right?"

"Of course," Bernie shrugged. "If there's a chance at a decent case I'll even put on a nylon spacesuit, charge up a phaser and march on the Emperor with you."

Mary blinked. "That's not… fine. Well, I don't know too much about it at the moment, just some rumours I heard from one of the forum members. But I'm going back tomorrow for the big last day of the con and I'll see what I can find out."

"Walker didn't give you any details?"

"He's being careful," Mary said, tracing a condensation droplet down her glass of wine. "While he's still a probationer with CID he can't take any chances. And he's worried about his exam. So I don't want to push it too much."

Liz thought Bernie would have a go about that one too, but her friend didn't go for the throat, for once.

"All right," Bernie said. "I'll leave the possible convention case in your hands. But if it looks like coming to something, make sure you put the WWC right in the middle of it. Celebrities have plenty of cash to throw about and we could do with some more income this month."

"Noted," Mary replied.

"Liz and I will focus on Ryan Porter and his family troubles. Liz, I want you to take the research side of things."

Liz agreed. "I've already made a start by looking up all the census data. There's a chance that this Marty person might be on there. Otherwise, I'm going to try the local Polish community groups. It's a slim hope, but I might find someone who knew him."

"Don't forget he went by a fake name. That's what Mrs Porter was told at least. Finn's going to ask around the trades for me. Ryan's mum said that Marty was a labourer and an HGV driver, so someone might have met him onsite. It's a tricky one though. Plenty of these guys didn't hang around. Chances are he's long gone. I've another call scheduled with Kaylie first thing tomorrow morning, so I'm going to tell her what we've got so far."

"Isn't it a bit of a conflict of interests having both Kaylie and Ryan for clients," Mary asked. "I mean, would Ryan want you sharing all this stuff about his family?"

"I'm not going to tell her any of the stuff about Ryan's dad," Bernie replied. "Just that he's not a cheating scumbag. That should cheer her up at least."

"What if we can't find Marty?" Liz asked. "I mean, it's not that easy if someone doesn't want to be found."

"We could try the Dark Web," Bernie said, saying the words to make the capital letters clear.

Liz snorted. "What the hell do you know about the dark web?"

"I read," Bernie said haughtily. "Criminals use it all the time, don't they. Maybe we could find avenues to explore that we don't have through legal channels. Have you ever been on the Dark Web?"

"What do you think," Liz clicked her tongue. "Honestly Bernie, what do you think I get up to in my spare time?"

"I ended up on a closed internet group for fans of the show *Firefly*," Mary piped up, shaking her head at the memory. "They really hated it being cancelled. It got pretty damn dark."

"Yes, Mary, that sounds exactly the same," Bernie snapped. "I can't believe none of you have tried to access the Dark Web. You know, it's where all the paedophile rings, human traffickers and contract killers hang out."

"You're on there all the time then are you?" Mary chuckled.

"Well, no, but I'm sure I could find it if I wanted to." Bernie said, running out of steam. "Maybe Walker can get us in there."

"I kind of think it's his job to keep civilians away from that sort of stuff," Mary pointed out.

"It's a shame," Bernie said. "I always fancied meeting a contract killer."

There was a moment of silence while Liz and Mary chose not to question that statement.

"What's our plan then?" Liz asked. "I mean, we've gone from one easy case to two pretty tricky ones. It feels like we're spread thin."

"We hustle. Mary will get us a foot in the door with the celebrity death threats, and even if you're not going to let me on the Dark Web we'll manage to find Ryan Porter's dad. And I haven't forgotten about your encounter with Kaylie's sister at the nursery either. If there's a killer on the loose among the yummy mummies then I reckon we're just the ones to uncover her."

"I'd better get going," Mary said, standing up. "The con starts at nine o'clock tomorrow morning and I've got to drive through to Glasgow."

"You and Walker will be enjoying having the house to yourselves."

"You're joking, right? He's stuck in a stake-out keeping an eye on the convention hotel. I did suggest I could sneak in but he turned me down." Mary shook her head. "So I'm going to go home and watch some more *Vampyra* for research. I don't suppose that justifies my streaming subscription as expenses?"

"Not a chance," Bernie replied. "I've just had a gas bill for this place. If we don't get many more cases this month then we'll have to take that O'Carroll case."

Liz shuddered. "Not the guy who's convinced the neighbour's dog is crapping on his doorstep?"

"That's the one. I know it'll violate our 'no dog poo' rule, but beggars can't be choosers."

"It also violates the 'no neighbourhood feuds' rule," Liz

reminded her.

"Then you lot better get your fingers out," Bernie said. "Unless Ryan Porter's dad turns out to be a secret Oligarch or a football club owner then we'll have to take what we can get."

With that stern warning, the meeting broke up. As Liz walked out of the door she noticed a chill in the air. The last of the summer warmth was leeching out of the atmosphere and it was starting to feel decidedly autumnal. Bernie might have a hard way of putting it, but her friend wasn't wrong. With three of them now partners in the business, liquidity was more important than rules about which cases they might take. Who knew what the future might hold, but Liz couldn't help hoping that it wouldn't include dog poo on a doorstep.

Chapter 11: Walker

The big police station at Govan was always busy and even Walker had to admit that the atmosphere was a bit more lively than Invergryff. The Invergryff station – often on the list for closure but limping along for the moment – shared a building with council staff and, latterly, several lawyers offices which was nothing if not convenient.

Govan police station on the other hand was a well-oiled machine, with sections for different divisions of policing. In Invergryff there were no permanent SCD officers and if there was a major crime then the detectives were pulled in from elsewhere. But Govan was part of Greater Glasgow and there was an entire floor of plain clothes officers.

"No vending machines though," Rav complained as they went inside.

"Didn't you eat at the convention?"

"Aye, but it was twelve quid for a baked potato. Nae chance."

Walker was about to reply when DI Macleod came back into the room.

"I've asked DS Magnusson to take us through the file for these threatening letters. He's been working on the social media side for us, poor lad. How did you get on with the actors?"

"They seem to be enjoying the attention," Walker said and

Rav nodded in agreement. "We've left a couple of uniforms on Strong and Alderick while we came over here."

"Any signs of any weirdos lurking about?" Macleod asked.

Rav burst out laughing. "How the hell would we know that? Sorry sir," he added when he saw the DI frown, "but today I've seen a dragon who was dating a zombie, a whole family dressed as chainsaw killers and so many superheroes I started to feel I should have had my underpants on outside my trousers."

Even Macleod couldn't resist a smile at that one. "You're saying it's difficult to spot our guy if he's there?"

"Impossible, more like."

"Thank you for your optimism."

A knock at the door announced DS Magnusson, a tall burly bloke with rugby player's ears. "I've got that report for you," the DS said.

"Great. Come in and you can talk us all through it."

After a quick round of introductions, Magnusson started to work through the information on his tablet.

"It's a tricky one," he began. "The letters themselves have barely any forensics other than flagging up a common paper and ink type. We're still looking into it, but they're unlikely to give us anything. So that's why I've been looking at the online stuff. I've been trying to see if any of the online threats match the wording of these notes."

"And did you find anything?" Macleod said eagerly.

"Oh, I found plenty. In just the last six weeks there were four hundred and seventy-eight messages sent either publicly or privately to the two civilians, three-quarters of them to Anetta Strong."

"Okay, then how many of these were serious threats?"

"Maybe ten per cent? These are the ones that specifically mention a threat to life. So that narrowed it down to thirty-seven threats that were worth a look. I tried to see if any of them used the phrase in the letters."

"You won't make it through another summer. Watch your back," Rav intoned.

"That's right. Unfortunately none of the online messages mentioned anything about summer."

Macleod groaned, but Magnusson was already holding up a hand.

"But there were three messages that used the words 'watch your back'. All of them sent to Miss Strong within the last two weeks."

Walker leaned forward, as did the others. "Who sent the messages?"

"If only it was that easy to find out. All three messages appeared in Anetta Strong's DMs from the same username 'spv1980'."

"Mean anything?"

"I guess it could give us his age?" Rav suggested.

"Can we ask the social media firm to tell us who he is?" Walker asked, although he had a feeling he already knew the answer.

"We can, but it's a bloody nightmare. Especially at this point where we've no evidence that anyone has carried out any threats. The best the company will do is shut down the account, and that only makes things worse."

"Because he'll start up the same things with a different username?"

"Exactly. Much better to keep an eye on him while he's still active."

Macleod tapped a pen on the table. "Do you have a transcript of what he said exactly?"

"Yep. I've uploaded it to the files. But it's interesting in one way. He's clearly a fan of the show. He starts off by complaining about a character who gets killed, someone called Gigorath?"

"Ah, Lord Gigorath. That's Vampyra's mentor in season one. They kill him off right at the end of the last episode. Pissed off lots of fans."

Every face in the room turned towards Walker.

"Sorry. Um. Didn't I mention I had seen the show?"

Magnusson cleared his throat. "Yeah, well the messages start off just a little wacky, like: *Gigorath will be avenged!* That sort of thing. And Miss Strong just ignores them, right? But then that seems to annoy him more. And then it gets personal. The next message is: *Gigorath was betrayed. You will be next.* And then when she ignored that one, he sends: *Don't underestimate me, bitch. You better watch your back in Glasgow.*"

That got a few raised eyebrows.

"It could just be an online troll," Macleod mused, rubbing his chin. "But that reference to Glasgow is interesting."

"That's what I thought Sir," Magnusson agreed.

"All right, keep digging. Get tech to put some pressure on the social media companies involved. Tell them that that we've had physical letters sent too. That might get them to open up their records."

Everyone in the room knew this was a forlorn hope, but Magnusson noted it down anyway.

"All right. This could still be a storm in a teacup, but we're going to treat it as a threat to life. Particularly where Anetta Strong is concerned. I want us to all head back over to the convention and I'm going to scare up as much uniform support as I can find. If our creep sees the lads in black walking around the convention, maybe he'll go off home and we won't have to worry about him."

Walker joined Rav as they packed up their bags and headed for the squad car. On the way out of the door, Macleod clapped him on the shoulder.

"Any news on the exam result yet?"

"No sir."

"I'm sure you'll be fine," the DI said.

"Yes sir," Walker replied, but he didn't meet his eye as they walked away.

Chapter 12: Mary

It was Mary's second day at the con and her second twenty-four hours without small people hanging off her side asking constant questions. Weirdly, she was starting to miss it. As she walked back through the automatic doors of the conference centre she wondered if it was possible to be under-stimulated. Mind you, the noise and sights of the con were almost as full-on as being with her four children. No one had been sick on her shoes yet though, so that was a definite plus.

Before the panels started she had a look around the bookshop, a dangerous place for anyone who loved books but still had a mortgage to pay. It was like one of those escape rooms that people seemed to love now, only no one was trying to get out, they had just accepted their fate. Mary managed to find the exit after twenty minutes and only had to sacrifice fifty quid on some obscure manga that she knew Vikki would love.

Next, she hurried over to a panel of women in sci-fi, featuring two famous authors and one slightly odd performance poet who kept claiming the 'rebirth' of feminism. Mary had felt put out that no one had told her it needed to be reborn, but she clapped politely along with everyone else at the end.

After this panel she wandered around, pretending that she wasn't looking for Walker. The thing was, when she'd gone home after the WWC meeting last night she had spent some time online looking up things like '*Vampyra* threats' and 'Anetta Strong letters' and to her surprise, she had found some messages on the forum talking about those very things.

The forum was a sub-set of a large sci-fi stack. It wasn't one that Mary had visited before as it had a bit of a reputation for not having any moderators. Because of this it was full of scammy messages and more racist/homophobic/generally unpleasant chat than your average internet site. But on this thread, the focus was on the *Vampyra* cast and the threats they had been receiving. It had started one week previously.

User FfBuckyohare 18/09/24: Did you hear that Little Miss Fangs is coming to Glasgow?

User 1980newjob 18/09/24: Aye, good luck to her. Won't be getting much of a welcome from me.

User Cash4gold 18/09/24: Any gold sitting at home doing nothing. Make sure you sell it well!

User Floflo 18/09/24: Surprised she'll show her face. Especially if the Toronto rumours are true.

User 1980newjob 19/09/24: Who gives a crap about Toronto. She's not going to make it out of Scotland.

User GIGlow 19/09/24: Ooh, harsh!

FfBuckyohare 19/09/24: Better watch, you'll get reported for that one Joe.

User 1980newjob 19/09/24: Like I care. Bitch is going down!

There was a gap of a few days, then the thread started up again.

User GIGlow 24/09/24: Heard someone's been sending Miss Fang some nastiograms. Any takers?

User FfBuckyohare 24/09/24: Nope

User GIGlow 25/09/24: No sign of 1920newjob right? Wonder if he's taken up a new job as a postie!!

User FfBuckyohare 25/09/24: Not funny

Thread closed.

It was all very interesting, not to mention majorly icky. Mary had copied the web page address and sent it over in an email to Walker. It was probably nothing, but if nothing else it showed just how much hate was out there for *Vampyra*'s main female lead. Not surprising that a beautiful woman should be the target of the fan's hate, but there was something a bit sinister about the fact that they were mentioning she was in Glasgow. Like the poor woman was being stalked or something.

Another panel, this time on Scottish fairytale that Mary very much enjoyed. Unfortunately, it led to her buying another two books of illustrated fairytales, but that could probably come out of the kids' education budget, right?

Then it was time for lunch, which was a problem. The easiest and cheapest option would have been to leave the convention centre and get something from one of the shops outside. But Mary was enjoying being in the 'bubble' too much so she braved the optimistically named 'refreshment area' which was a scrum of overpriced food stalls with far too many people trying to fight for a seat. She managed to find a gyro wrap – twelve bloody quid, Bernie would have had a conniption – and found a tiny table up against the wall to perch at. She brought out her phone – the best friend of the solo diner – and started to plan her afternoon.

"Is this seat taken?"

A pretty woman with a soft transatlantic accent and a huge cup of coffee stood beside her.

"Please, sit down," Mary said, scooting over to make room.

The woman grinned at her, "it's like the zoo in here."

"Right," Mary replied. "Only instead of animals it's robots and princesses."

"Exactly."

Mary glanced at the woman and realised there was something familiar about her.

"Would I be being an arse if I asked if I knew you?" she said, unable to keep it inside. "You look really familiar."

"Oh, I'm a make-up artist. I've been on a few panels here."

"OMG, You're Tiana Schmidt!" Mary couldn't help but blurt it out. "You work on *Vampyra*, right?"

"Yeah," Tiana sipped at her giant cup. "I did spot your hoodie."

"I should have realised," Mary replied. "Your eyelashes are beautiful by the way."

"Oh, thanks," the woman beamed at her. "Of course, I have to keep the really good stuff for my clients. Take a look at the lashes Anetta's got on today. They're fifty quid a pop."

"Wow," Mary was genuinely impressed. She had to pull the clumps off her five year old mascara every time she used it. No wonder the celebs always looked so good.

"You know, someone was saying that Anetta had been getting some threatening letters," Mary said, the investigator in her unable to give up the opportunity to ask questions.

"So they say. I haven't seen any evidence of them. She probably sent them to herself for the drama," Tiana added, then clapped a hand to her mouth. "Please don't put that on social media."

Mary smiled. "Of course not. Did you do the make-up for the half-dragons too?" she asked, trying to put the woman back at ease.

"Some of it," Tiana nodded. "Some of it is added with CGI, the horns and stuff. But I do all the facial scales."

"Awesome." Something else about the woman was ringing a bell. "Hang on, you didn't work on *Space Rover Seven*, did you? I think I remember seeing your name."

Tiana laughed and actually slapped her thigh which might be the most American thing Mary had ever seen anyone do. "I didn't think anyone remembered that show. Yeah, that was one of my first gigs."

"I loved that series!" Mary could barely contain her excitement. *SR7* had been one of her first sci-fi obsessions, an ill-fated series which followed an alien detective solving crimes on a decaying space station in a distant galaxy. In hindsight, the scripts had been hokey at best, but the make-up had been excellent.

"There was a fish lady," Mary said, remembering the character vividly. "Her name was Xhova, I think."

"Xhoba," Tiana corrected. "I did all her make-up and prosthetics."

"I dressed up as her for Halloween one year. I stuck on the gills myself with superglue. It took ages to get all the glue off my skin."

This earned her a roaring laugh from the other woman. "That's brilliant. What did you say your name was again?"

"Mary. Mary Plunkett."

"You've made my day Mary."

Something occurred to Mary. "Would it be too geeky to ask you to sign my hoodie for me?"

"I'd love to. I'll do it on the back so I don't mess up the artwork."

A pen was produced from somewhere and Mary felt the light scratches as Tiana wrote on her back.

"Thank you so much!"

"You're welcome."

By the time Mary had said goodbye and Tiana had wandered off in search of her crew, it was nearly time for another panel. Mary was dying to know what Tiana had written but she had to make it to the other side of the arena and there was no way she was going to be late. A popular fantasy author was giving a talk and the rumour was he was going to spill the beans on why his most recent novel still hadn't been released a decade after it had been written. Mary, like everyone else at the convention, was hoping for some juicy gossip.

In reality, the publisher had sent an agent to sit next to the author, a bit like a bodyguard but more like a minder. Whenever the bearded man mentioned his latest book the agent gave a demure little cough and the subject was gently changed. Right up until the closing comments, where the author lost his temper.

"Oh, and the problem with the new book seems to be that the main character is too gay. At least that's what the right-wing arsehole head of marketing told me. So you can pass that one on to the press. I'll be publishing the damned thing myself, just in time for Christmas."

The minder's jaw dropped and the whole room applauded. Great fun. Mary was still laughing to herself when she filed out of the room into a short film screening. Three short films later of varying quality later, it was time for the big *Vampyra* panel.

Yesterday's panel had just been a forty minute session, but due to the show's sudden popularity, the organisers had given them an hour-long slot to close out the conference. Mary had splurged on a VIP ticket for this one, which was worth it for the guaranteed seat at the front. Although it did mean she had to walk slightly awkwardly past the queue or normal punters waiting to get in.

She found her allocated seat and was pleased to see she was on the right hand side with a good view of the full stage. There was no sign of her elf friend from the previous day, but she chatted with her neighbours, who were, unsurprisingly, all huge *Vampyra* fans.

"Who do you think the surprise guest will be?" A girl with a high ponytail asked her.

"Well, Stefan turned up yesterday, so I guess it might be him."

"Yeah, but he's been added to the official program, so I'm hoping it might be someone else."

It turned out that ponytail girl was right. When the lights dimmed and the panellists walked onto the stage, there was someone new. Anetta came first, of course, and this time she had donned a particularly striking set of *Vampyra* armour, all shining scales and black lace. Her famous dragon-scale tattoo snaked across her collarbones. Alderick came behind her, waving and blowing kisses to the crowd. The writer, Tim Errin was next, and he seemed to be in the exact same clothes from yesterday. And then there was a surprising face, one that got several woops and cheers from the crowd.

"Wow, how the hell did they get Gigorath to come?"

The Shakespearean actor Fletcher Moon filled the stage, not just with his bulk which was not inconsiderable, but also with his energy, lifting his arms to embrace the cheers from the crowd. It was indeed a shock appearance, considering that his character Lord Gigorath had died at the end of the last season. The rumour going around had been that Moon had been sacked from the show, but Mary reckoned he couldn't have been too upset if he was willing to appear on the panel.

The chair arrived, a veteran actress who had appeared as a guest star on the second season as the voice of a sentient tree. Sheila O'Hare was her name and Mary thought she was a good chair, both happy to let each person answer questions and not afraid to cut them off if they were babbling. Anetta gave her a filthy look at one point when she was trying to promote one of her perfume brands, but apart from that it was all quite amicable.

It wasn't until half an hour in that something went wrong. There was a brief moment when Mary thought she could hear a creaking sound, like someone had opened an old door. Then there was a flash and she saw movement on the left hand side of the stage. One of the huge lighting rigs, all twelve feet of it was collapsing.

A moment later it was down, metal screeching and pieces of plastic and glass strewing themselves over the stage. People in the audience started screaming and standing up from their chairs. Like the others, Mary felt panic rise in her chest.

"Stay calm! If you all start running we'll have a problem." It was Walker's voice. He had jumped onto the stage and grabbed the microphone. Only now did Mary realise that the people on stage had been narrowly missed by the debris, although they all looked shaken up.

Anetta had been closest to the collapse and she was lying on the floor, but moving at least. Stefan had got out of his seat and crouched down beside her.

"She's all right, thank God, she's okay." Stefan pulled Annetta into his arms. Mary was mildly irritated to note that even mid-swoon the actress looked as pristine as ever. Like a still from a period drama.

"Everyone stand back," Walker was saying. "Evacuate the room please."

Mary was torn between wanting to obey her boyfriend and not cause any more trouble for the harassed-looking security staff, and her natural curiosity as to what had happened. It might have killed the cat, but Mary was a private investigator by profession and nature so while everyone else was filing out of the door at the back of the room, she slid over to the side curtains and eased her way through to backstage.

Here there was more damage, where the lighting rig had been attached to some sort of metal scaffolding it had swept down and was lying in shattered pieces. It was oddly quiet, although the air was thick with dust and plastic fumes.

Under one corner of the scaffolding was a pile of coats where someone had left...

Mary took a pace forward. That wasn't a pile of coats. There was something... someone...

There was a scream that might have been her own and suddenly Walker was there, his arm around her.

"Is that..."

He pushed past her to crouch next to the figure. He pressed his fingers to her neck, then shook his head.

"She's already cold."

"But —"

He stood up and took her arm. "I'm sorry, but you need to get out of here. It's a crime scene and the next few minutes are going to be crucial. You understand? I love you, but you can't be here."

"I understand. I just can't believe that Tiana is dead."

"Tiana?"

"The make-up woman. I was chatting to her earlier. I'm pretty sure that's her. I mean, I can't see her face but that's what she was wearing." To Mary's annoyance, she felt her shoulders tremble.

"Find yourself somewhere to get a cup of tea," Walker said, speaking softly now. "You've had a bad shock. Sit down and look after yourself, okay? I'll call as soon as I can."

Feeling numb, Mary nodded her ascent. Stumbling slightly she made her way back out through the curtain. On the way she passed the actors on stage who seemed to be comparing bruises. She couldn't look at them. Couldn't do anything until she found a quiet bench and settled herself down for a jolly good cry.

Chapter 13: Bernie

It only took one look at Mary's face when she arrived at Bernie's house on Sunday morning for Bernie to go into full nurse mode.

"Tea," she said firmly as she led the shivering woman into her kitchen. "With two sugars. And two of Finn's chocolate biscuits that he's been hiding under the sink. Then you can tell me what happened."

Bernie watched as the colour returned to her friend's face.

"Sorry," Mary said once she had downed the tea and one of the biscuits. "I just didn't know where else to go. It was all so horrible."

Even though Bernie had often criticised Mary for being a 'wet lettuce', she knew that her friend was not prone to hysterics.

"Tell me what happened."

After a couple of false starts, Mary managed to recount the events at the convention and the sad discovery of Tiana Schmidt's body.

"And you had met the woman earlier that day?"

"Yeah. We shared a table in the café and I was a total fan-girl over her," Mary sniffed. "She was nice."

"She didn't seem worried about anything? Nervous?"

Mary shook her head. "No. I've been thinking about it ever since I found her. She didn't seem like someone worried for her life. In fact, she was talking about the letters that had been sent to the cast and she was laughing about them. She thought it was all a big joke."

"But it wasn't."

"No. I can't help but feel that Tiana was collateral damage. Whoever damaged that lighting rig was trying to hit the people on stage. Maybe Tiana caught them or something."

Bernie had learned to trust Mary's instincts. Liz was always analytical: twenty years of being an accountant meant that she dealt in facts and absolutes. Bernie herself was what you might call an investigative bludgeon: she forced her way into people's lives until they gave up their secrets, whether they wanted to or not. But Mary was something else. She was good at reading people, intelligent, and the sort of person that people always underestimated. In some ways, the most natural investigator of the three of them.

"Could be," Bernie said after a moment's thought. "Although, didn't you say that Walker said the body was cold?"

Mary shuddered again.

"Eat that other biscuit," Bernie said firmly.

"Yes ma'am," her friend rolled her eyes but she put the biscuit in her mouth anyway.

"My point was that if the body was cold," Bernie pressed on, "then she might have been dead for a while. It might be unconnected to what happened on stage."

Mary rubbed at her forehead. "If she was killed beforehand, then it changes the complexion of the case. It means that any of the people on the panel could have killed her. If she was killed just before the rig went down then they all have alibis."

"Then we've got to hope that your boyfriend and the rest of the coppers do a thorough job on the time of death. Make sure you get all the info out of him you can."

The other woman made a face. "You know that Walker can't tell me too much."

"Just use your charms. I'm sure you can think of something to change his mind."

"Ugh, you're making it all sound very sleazy," Mary wrinkled her nose. "And besides, if we want to get paid for the investigation we'll have to go down a more official route."

"True. I'll see if Macleod can do anything for us." Bernie still had the DI's number from when they had consulted for the police before. It had to be worth a shot. And even if they weren't paid, it couldn't hurt to keep an eye on the investigation. Even if they didn't get paid for solving murders, word got around. And in their line of business, reputation was everything.

"How's Liz getting on with the Kaylie and Ryan nuptials," Mary asked. Bernie was not always the most intuitive, but she got the feeling her friend wanted to change the subject for a while.

"Not great. We're looking up all the different avenues we can to try to find Marty. I've got Finn putting the word out with the guys on the tools, but it doesn't sound like anyone remembers him. Not surprising really. Labouring is a young man's game and most of the lads who were around thirty-odd years ago are doing other things now."

"What exactly did Ryan's mother tell you?"

"The delightful Mrs Claire Porter remembers very little about the man. Oh, except that he gave her a fake name, which she didn't seem worried about enough if you ask me. I don't suppose your boyfriend would go and check some police records for me? Look into any Poles with criminal records lurking about at the time."

Mary sighed. "I think he might be a little busy at the moment."

"That's what I thought. Don't worry, I'm sure I can persuade one of the other plods to have a look for me. No one changes their name for an innocent reason. I bet that our Marty has a record as long as his arm. Either that or a half dozen wives scattered all over Europe."

"That's reaching a bit, isn't it?"

"The only thing we know about him is that he was happy to leave someone pregnant and bugger off back to his own country. Not exactly the basis of a strong character."

"True," Mary nodded. "But we only know one side of the story."

"Sometimes there only is one," Bernie said firmly. "Or only

one that matters at any rate. How are you feeling now? All right or more carbs?"

Her friend let out a long breath. "Maybe some more carbs?"

"Coming right up."

Chapter 14: Liz

Liz's Sunday had mainly been spent tracking down where Linda Novak worked. The woman had been on her mind not just because she was Kaylie Michelson's sister, but due to her odd remark at the nursery gates. After a close examination of her social media, Liz discovered that Linda worked as a beautician in the centre of Invergryff. Excellent, Liz thought. Time to get my nails done.

After a quick call to the salon to make sure that Linda was working that day, Liz drove into town and parked up nearby. She walked in with a spring in her step. She hadn't had her nails done for ages, and Bernie would definitely have to pay this one on expenses if it turned into a WWC case. A win/win scenario.

The only snag occurred when she entered the salon.

"Hi, I phoned up about a last minute nail appointment?"

A friendly woman with an orange face smiled big teeth at her. "Of course, you've with Susan. She'll take you over in the back there."

"Oh, I'd heard that Linda was good. Is she not free?"

The woman frowned. "I think there's been a mix-up. Linda does brows, not nails. She is free though if you want?"

Liz felt her mouth go dry. She had only had her eyebrows

done twice and neither had been a happy experience. Both times it had taken weeks before she could look at herself in the mirror without wincing.

"Oh, well, I'm not sure…"

The other woman gently patted her arm. "Might be nice to freshen up those brows, eh?"

Liz was so shocked that she allowed herself to be led around the corner to the beauty room where the tables covered in towels reminded her of a torture room. Could have been worse, she told herself as she sat down in a padded chair. Could have been a bikini wax.

"Want a look at the pictures?" Linda Novak clipped over on her high heels and presented a laminated folder of eyebrow pictures. Liz flicked through, pretending she knew what she was doing. Some of the eyebrows were startling, of the 'more is more' persuasion. Liz had first done her eyebrows in the nineties, where they had to be plucked within an inch of their lives. So the furry slugs on offer were quite alarming.

"I want to keep it natural," she said desperately. "So I guess just a little bit of shaping."

"Hmmn," Linda drew closer so that she could stare at Liz's forehead. "I think that might be for the best. Is this your first time here?"

"Yes."

"And you needed a last minute slot?"

Liz swallowed. She suddenly felt vulnerable with Linda interrogating her. She was aware of how exposed she was lying back with her eyes closed as Linda applied some sort of sticky substance to her brows.

"Oh, I just felt like treating myself. I thought I might get my nails done too. A wee bit of pampering, you know?"

That seemed to satisfy Linda who nodded. "Nothing like a wee treat. We do lip filler too, if you want to look really nice."

Liz tried to conceal a shudder. "No thanks. Not really my thing."

This earned her a grunt of disappointment.

"It's nice to have a chance to relax," Liz said, in spite of her fingers clawing into the armrests. "I've got a toddler at home, so I don't get much opportunity to be on my own."

"Oh have you? I've got a wee one at home too. He's three."

"My Isioma is only two." Liz swallowed as something sharp pulled at the corner of her eye. "You don't use the new nursery on St George Place, do you? I think I might have seen you there."

"Aye. I've one at the school on the corner and wee Connor is in the nursery."

"That's right. This is going to sound weird, but I saw you going into the nursery on Friday and you seemed, well, kind of pissed off with one of the other mums."

"Did I?"

There was a scorched smell in the air that Liz was determined to pretend hadn't anything to do with what was happening on her forehead.

"I only remember because... well, you said that someone was a killer."

"Did I?" There was definitely an 'atmosphere' in the room now. "And you were lugging in, were you?"

"No, no." Liz swallowed. Probably best to be honest or risk permanent facial damage. "Actually yes. I'm a private investigator you see, so it's kind of my job."

"God, you're not part of those con artists that my sisters' using are you?"

"Umm?"

"I see." Ms Novak pulled back and Liz was rather glad to not be staring into the woman's nostrils for a change. "You didn't just turn up here for an emergency appointment, did you?"

"No. Not exactly. I am part of the team that your sister hired, but we're not con artists. Not anything like that. We're trying to help Kaylie."

Linda folded her arms. "You think you're helping her, do you? Getting her back together with that waste of space Ryan."

"It's what she wants," Liz said, remembering Bernie's speech about how Kaylie would be better getting a dog than Ryan for a husband.

"And Kaylie always gets what she wants," Linda spat out. "That's the bloody trouble you see. She's always been the favourite daughter, always had everything handed to her on a plate, and then when Ryan chucked her, she just couldn't believe it. Total denial. How could anyone break up with perfect Kaylie."

"That's not the nicest thing to say about your sister, is it?"

"You got a sister?"

"No."

"Then you don't have a bloody clue."

There were a few minutes of silence where Linda went back to doing things to Liz's poor assaulted eyebrows.

"From our initial investigations," Liz said, filling the silence as much as anything else. "It looks like Ryan had a decent reason for delaying the wedding. We're hoping to get it sorted so that the wedding can go ahead soon."

Linda sighed. "Well, that's great then. At least it'll stop her from going on about it."

A random comment from Bernie made its way into Liz's brain. "You wouldn't… there wasn't anything between you and Ryan was there? I mean, he says that's not why he is postponing the wedding but…"

"Do I look like the sort of ho-bag who would steal her sister's man?"

"No, not at all, it was just a thought."

Linda withdrew from the chair and crossed her arms. "That's us done then."

"Good," Liz said, keeping up the fake cheer.

"Want to take a look in the mirror."

Oh dear. Liz supposed there was no point in putting it off. She got up from the chair and walked over to the large mirror.

"They're, well…" Liz peered closer. "They're quite nice actually."

"What, did you think I would mess them up just cause you've come in here being a cheeky beggar? I'm a professional."

"Of course," Liz cringed again. "Well, thank you for speaking to me. But I'm still wondering about that thing you said at the nursery."

"It's got nothing to do with Kaylie and Ryan."

"No, I get that. It's just, well, you seemed so angry. And people don't throw around the word killer, not unless they're pretty certain about it."

Linda wrinkled despite the botox on her forehead. "You really are a nosy bitch, aren't you?"

"It's sort of in the job description," Liz said with a shrug. "And it felt like you might need to talk to someone. I can't get away, so why not let it be me?"

That earned Liz another eye-roll, but at last Linda spoke.

"All right then. The fifth of October, 2022. A car crash on the motorway just outside Invergryff. Go and look up the articles about it. Let me know then if you think I'm right to call Perrie Mellworth a killer."

Chapter 15: Walker

The trainee detectives Walker and Rav were certainly getting the full experience of being a detective, including the part where you get a bollocking from a superior officer.

"You were meant to prevent a bloody murder," Detective Chief Inspector Yvonne Allan said, her wiry frame taught with tension. The DCI was based in South Glasgow and Walker had never met her before. So far, it wasn't the best first meeting.

"What the hell were you lot doing, eh? Getting autographs?"

Macleod stayed quiet until the storm was over. He had warned them before she arrived that Allan's 'bark was worse than her bite' but the woman was practically growling at them.

"It's an arena with ten thousand people, boss," Macleod held out his hands, "there was only so much the three of us could do."

DCI Allan shrugged, which Walker took to be a slight acknowledgement of Macleod's point. "Tell me again what happened."

Rav took over the narrative this time. "We were at the back of the room with the security officers. This was the final panel of the day and the two victims of the threats were on the stage. The panel had been going for twenty-five minutes when the lighting rig collapsed."

"And at that point you didn't know about the death of Miss Schmidt?"

Walker shook his head. "No. We thought the danger was to the people on stage. Rav and I moved forward and made sure that the people up there were safe."

"There were some minor injuries, is that right?"

"Sort of," Walker frowned. He still wasn't sure exactly what had happened. "It looked at first like Anetta Strong was injured but she was... well, it seemed a bit like she was playing up for attention."

"She was loving it," Rav added. "And people were taking pictures of her fainting and stuff. But when we went to question her she said she was fine."

"Two other people on stage were hit by pieces of metal, but none bad enough to require anything more than first aid treatment."

"And while all of this was going on," DCI Allan tapped her fingers on her elbow. "While this was happening there was a victim just behind the curtain. Who found her."

Ah. Time for the awkward bit.

"It was my partner. I mean, my girlfriend. She was attending the con."

Walker cringed at the way the DCI's jaw tightened. "Your girlfriend discovered our victim? That's some coincidence."

"She's actually a private investigator."

Allan pinched the bridge of her nose. "Of all the stupid, irresponsible –"

Walker's guardian angel arrived in the guise of a sweaty-looking uniformed constable.

"Sorry, Gov, but the panel members are getting quite agitated. They're saying that if you don't start the interviews soon then they're going to leave."

"All right, let's wrap this up so we can go see them. Walker, this conversation is not over, but there are a dozen people to interview, not to mention all the mobile phone footage we're going to have to go through tonight. I need everyone to focus on the case, right?"

"Right," Walker replied, giving her his most reassuring smile. She did not return it. "I could start with the members of the panel. I've already met Anetta Strong when I was organising her close protection, so I could begin with her interview."

"Sounds like you were guarding the wrong person."

Walker cleared his throat. "As we understood it, the letters had specifically targeted the actors. We weren't expecting the make-up artist to be at risk."

"Maybe it wasn't targeted at all," the DCI suggested. "Until we know the cause of death and what actually happened at the crime scene, we don't know if Schmidt was merely in the wrong place at the wrong time."

Macleod was nodding in agreement. "It could be that we have an opportunist assailant. They just wanted to get someone connected with the show."

"What I don't like about that idea is that it means we're not dealing with someone that has a rational grudge. We're dealing with someone who just wants to cause harm and fear to as many people as possible."

"It has already worked," Walker said, his mouth set in a grimace. "Security are treating it like a terrorist incident. The whole arena has been shut down and cleared."

"And our suspect has been cleared out along with all the rest," the DCI said.

"It looks like it," Macleod agreed. "But with a risk to the public and ten thousand people in the building, there wasn't any other choice."

"Understood," the DCI said, although she still didn't look happy. "There's going to be a hell of a lot of media scrutiny on this. After the Arena bombing in Manchester and the threats made at Taylor Swift concerts, the politicians are going to be very sensitive to any suggestion of terrorist involvement. The sooner we can narrow this down to one lone guy with a grudge against the victim, the better."

No one felt they could add to that comment. Walker knew as well as the others that the press were going to go nuts about this one. It was a race against time to get any investigating done before the circus moved in.

"Right. What are our first actions?" DCI Allan asked Macleod.

"I've got the cast and crew of *Vampyra* – that's Schmidt's workmates – sequestered in one of the spare conference rooms. From what the constable said we better interview them first, establish a timeline and then let them go. They've already been waiting a while and obviously they're only here voluntarily."

"Are any of them likely suspects?"

"Not on the surface." Macleod shrugged his shoulders. "But who can tell? I think we have to treat everyone that had the opportunity to kill Tiana as being a possible suspect."

The DCI let out another groan. "That's another problem. Until we get a firm time of death, we can't even start ruling people out. Every person that was in the arena today is a suspect."

Walker and Rav left the DCI grumbling at Macleod and hurried off to start the interviews.

"I'll take Anetta," Walker said, "she knows who I am already."

"Sure, you take the beautiful movie star. How selfless of you," Rav said, making a rude face at him.

Honestly, there was nothing wrong with wanting to spend time with a face like Anetta's, but that wasn't why Walker wanted to interview her. When they had met earlier she had struck him as ambitious and happy to do anything to get her name out there. Her social media was full of advertisements for products disguised as 'brand collaborations' and none of her co-stars seemed to like her much. To Walker she seemed just the sort of person who might get rid of anyone standing in her way. He just had to find a motive for why she might have seen Tiana as a threat.

"Sure, but apart from the biggest ego, who do you think we should speak to first?"

That made Walker pause for a second. "Let's find out who was last to see Tiana. Or at least, who will admit to it."

"Sounds good." Rav opened the door and immediately a dozen people started talking a hundred miles an hour. The lead actress pushed her way to the front.

"I want to get my interview over with," Anetta said. She was flanked by two people, her agent and another, nervous-looking woman.

"I realise that, Ms Strong," Rav said, puffing out his chest to assert his authority. "And my colleague here will be interviewing you shortly. But I'd really like to speak to the last people to see Tiana before she died. Did anyone see her after four o'clock?"

There was a murmur of conversation, then two people raised their hands. One was Stefan Alderick and the other was a skinny man with a goatee that Walker hadn't met before.

"All right, you two come with me," Walker told them. "The others will be interviewed by Sergeant Sangar here and his team."

There were some grumbles at that, but everyone started

moving towards the appropriate person. Walker nodded to Alderick and the other man and led them out of the room. He took them into a small side room that the conference centre had let them use as part of the investigation.

"Do we need a lawyer," Alderick asked in a half-joking, half-serious tone.

"This is just a preliminary interview," Walker explained. "At the moment we're just trying to work out what happened and when. Anything you can tell us will be a great help."

"I only spoke to her for five minutes," the goatee-d man said, his words coming out in a nervous rush.

"All right. Can I take your name first?"

"It's Colin Barrie. I work in tech support here at the convention hall. I do the lighting and the IT for the stages."

Walker leaned forward, making the man jump. "You're responsible for the lighting rig that fell?"

"Yes. Well, no. I mean, I didn't make it fall. Honest!" Sweat was gathering on the man's temple.

"Let's just establish the facts first," Walker told him. Although, if he started acting any more guilty, he would have to interview the lad under caution for his own good. "When did you set up the lighting platform?"

"On Saturday morning. It wasn't moved after that because that area was only used for panels. I just had to go and adjust the individual lights in between."

"So when was the last time you touched it?"

"Just before the panel started. The technology is kind of old-school, so I have to manually climb up to the top of the platform and check all the lights. Once they are all in position I can operate them from a remote control at the back of the room."

Walker made sure that he was recording all of this. "I'll need you to write all this up in an official statement, but I'd like to understand what happened for now. When you adjusted the lights before the panel there was nothing unusual about the rig?"

"Nothing at all. It was fine. The whole thing is tethered to a weight. It shouldn't have been possible for it to fall down like that."

The man looked like he was close to tears.

"And you had no idea that there was a body behind the curtain.

"No!" He wailed, "I don't need to go back there. In fact, that's where the panellists were getting changed, so we weren't meant to go anywhere near it. I swear!"

After another five minutes of the man pleading innocence and Walker managed to get rid of him. He sent Barrie to one of the uniformed constables to take his official statement, but if he was guilty, then the man was a better actor than the entire cast of *Vampyra* put together.

Besides, what motive would the man have to kill the make-up

artist? Walker made a note to check out Colin Barrie's online presence and see if he had a penchant for sending threatening messages to people, but he knew it was a waste of time.

The interview with Alderick was much quicker. The actor barely knew Tiana – there was a second make-up artist who did the male leads on set – and hadn't seen or spoken to her that day. He was friendly enough, but clearly eager to get back to his hotel room and out of the convention where people were still asking for his autograph, even though a woman was dead. Walker released him as soon as he good.

Once Alderick left, Walker checked his phone and waved over to Rav.

"You all right?"

"Yeah. Look, I'd really like to check in on Mary. She found the body after all and I don't like the idea of leaving her at home alone."

Rav rolled his eyes, but he didn't argue the point. "All right. I'll make excuses for you if the bosses turn up."

"Thanks," Walker said. His heart was already growing lighter as he made his way out of the conference centre and into his car.

Chapter 16: Mary

By the time Mary left Bernie's place it was late on Sunday night and she felt like a worn-out dish rag. Bernie Paterson had surprised her. She hadn't given Mary a telling off for being a 'wet lettuce', nor had she reminded Mary that she should be immune to dead bodies as a private investigator. Instead, Bernie had been patient, had listened to Mary's horror at discovering poor Tiana lying on the ground, and had plied her with tea. When Mary had stopped shaking then Bernie had popped a frozen pizza in the oven for dinner.

"It's got to be bad if you're willing to eat carbs," Mary had told her.

"Oh, that's for you. I don't eat that stuff. It's four hundred calories a slice!"

As Mary had eaten her way through the pizza, she had found her initial shock and horror receding. She was able to talk about Tiana in the way she would now think of her: an unfortunate victim in a murder case.

"I'm going to get in touch with Macleod," Bernie had decided once only crumbs remained. "We've partnered with him before and the fact that you were on the scene means that you are uniquely placed to help."

Mary wasn't so sure. She knew that a case like this would bring a lot of publicity for the force. Even if Macleod was willing to consult with them in private, a public partnership with the

WWC might be quite another matter. But she was too tired to argue, and eventually made her excuses and left.

"Don't you stay up all night watching the news reports," Bernie had warned her as she walked out of the house. "Try and get a good sleep. I promise you'll feel better in the morning."

Excellent advice, Mary thought as she made herself a camomile tea in her own kitchen. But not that easy to follow. She stared, unseeing at the walls of her home. It wouldn't be so bad if the kids were home. Then the house would be full of laughter and screams and kiddie chatter. But now it was silent. As silent as the grave.

Stop being so maudlin, she told herself. She looked down at her *Vampyra* sweatshirt and felt the tears threaten her eyes again. Wet lettuce indeed. She hurried upstairs, changed into her pyjamas and wrapped her cosiest dressing gown around herself.

Maybe it was time for some mindless TV. Something to distract her from the day. She put on her telly and her favourite streaming service, only to be confronted by a trailer for the new *Vampyra* series. She flicked it off. Now was not the time.

She was just considering making her way to bed when the doorbell rang. Mary looked down at her dressing gown.

"Crap." She just had to hope it wasn't a stranger. She had once spent half an hour chatting to a local election candidate without realising she had changed into her Ghostbusters pyjamas at three in the afternoon. The promised party leaflets had never materialised.

Mary went to the front door and pulled it open a crack, then smiled when she saw who was standing there.

"I'm so sorry I couldn't get away before," Walker said, pulling her into a hug so quickly that she nearly stepped out of her fluffy tribble slippers.

"It's all right," Mary said, her voice muffled against his chest. She felt the tears prick her eyes and blinked them away. She didn't want him to think she was some silly civilian shocked by a dead body.

"No, it's not."

"No, I guess it isn't. Why didn't you use your key?" Mary said, leading him inside.

"I thought you might be annoyed that I took so long to come over."

"Of course not. I understand that you had to… that you had to stay with the body."

Walker kept his eyes on hers. "I'm so sorry you saw her like that."

Mary nodded. "I know. Come on, I'll put the kettle on."

"Hang on, let me grab some stuff from the car."

She was glad of the few minutes to compose herself. Not that Walker would care if she was a blubbering mess, of course.

But their relationship was more complicated than boyfriend/girlfriend. She wanted him to think of her as a colleague, if that was possible. A fellow investigator at least.

Walker walked in with a bouquet of sunflowers. Their cheery yellow faces always made her smile.

"Thank you," Mary said, "Although I don't know if I've got a vase big enough."

"That's all right, let's just leave them in the sink."

He plonked them in and they both admired the effect.

"Like something in a shiny magazine," Mary said. "Except for all the kids' plastic cups on the drainage board. Do you think they spoil the aesthetic?"

"Nah." He pulled her in for another hug. "Let's get that cuppa and we can talk about everything that happened."

Five minutes later they curled up on the sofa together with tea and a packet of chocolate biscuits from Mary's secret cupboard that the kids couldn't reach.

"Kids not back yet?" Walker asked once they were settled.

"Long weekend remember? Camping with their dad and Stephanie."

"Of course, how could I forget. You've not had anyone message yet wanting to go home?"

"From the kids? Of course not, they'll be having a ball. I half-thought I might have one from Stephanie though. I'm not sure she's quite realised what she's let herself in for. Did I tell you that Peter insisted on bringing Gary?"

"The stick insect?" Walker shuddered. "I thought that thing died."

"Nah, false alarm. It was just sleeping. It's kind of hard to tell really when you think about it. Anyway, I hope Stephanie likes bugs."

"Giant bugs," Walker muttered. "I never thought it was possible to develop a new phobia in my thirties but seeing that thing on the pillow that day…"

"Yeah." It hadn't been her son's finest moment. Although even Mary had had to stifle a smile at Walker's leaping out of the bed screaming wearing only his boxers.

"How is the investigation going?" Mary asked.

"Badly. No suspects, we don't even know cause of death yet. And all five thousand people at the event had the opportunity to carry out the murder. If that's what it was."

"I can't believe I spoke to her just before she… It's so sad."

"Do you want to tell me what happened?"

"I already gave a statement."

Walker squeezed her hand. "I don't mean an official statement. I mean, give me the impression of what you saw today. You've always had a good instinct for noticing things other people don't. I reckon you'll have spotted more than any officer there, including me."

If only she had the confidence in herself that he had in her. Mary sipped her tea and thought for a moment. "All right. Well, I didn't notice anything off with her when we had our wee chat. If anything, she was more friendly than most of the people there. I totally fan-girled all over her and she didn't seem to mind. Then she signed my – oh!"

Mary jumped to her feet and ran up the stairs, ignoring Walker's confused shouts behind her. She reached into the laundry basket and pulled out her hoodie, turning it over to look at the back.

To Mary, from your number one fan, Tiana.

What a lovely, funny, silly thing to write. By the time Walker came in, Mary was blubbering all over again. But when he pulled her close, it didn't seem to matter quite so much.

Chapter 17: Bernie

Bernie was a little disappointed that by Monday morning all the Stormwarriors and Doctor Whats had left for the weekend. The conference centre had that 'living room after the party vibe'. The only clue that something unusual had gone on was a few early paparazzi setting up their cameras outside. That and the police tent out front. That was a stark reminder of the sad events of the previous day. It was also, for Bernie and Mary, something to be avoided.

"Let's go around the back," Bernie said as they approached the large, warehouse-style building.

"They're not going to let us in," Mary moaned. Bernie ignored her friend's pessimism. There was always a way to get in anywhere, you just had to learn how to assert yourself. She had been glad when Mary had turned up first thing that morning, ready to drive them over to Glasgow. After the shock of the day before, she wasn't sure what state her friend would be in. But as usual, Mary Plunkett had surprised her, in a positive way.

"I shouldn't have let you talk me into this," Mary muttered as they strode past the journalists trying not to draw any attention.

"Why? Are you worried about going back to where that poor lass was killed?"

"No. I'm worried about what my boyfriend is going to say

when we turn up at his place of work like two bad pennies."

Huh. Bernie hadn't thought about it that way, but it didn't change her mind. Walker was Mary's problem, not hers. They walked around the back of the building, pretending they were just out for a stroll. Unlike the front which was all shiny tiles and fancy paving, the back was a jumble of goods vehicles and worker's huts.

"Hang on a sec," Bernie said before they walked any further. She reached into her back and brought out her secret weapon.

"What the hell is this?" Mary asked, taking a bright blue tabard and holding it in front of her. "Did you nick these from when you worked in the care home?"

"Maybe," Bernie said, pulling it on. "But it's bog standard uniform for cleaners and I'll bet it'll get us in."

Mary pulled it over her top and pulled a face. "As long as you're not expecting me to do any mopping. These are my good shoes."

"Really? Are you sure? Anyway, this is only to get us in. Once we're inside we'll find our crime scene, speak to our witnesses and be on our merry way."

"Sure."

"Oh, and stick this on," Bernie pulled out a dusty-looking hat. "Half of the police in there will know what you look like."

Mary's lip curled as she put on the cap. "What's the logo?"

"Some football team or other. Now shut up and let me do the talking."

Mary might have mumbled something like 'how could I stop you' but Bernie was already striding forward.

"This door is restricted," a voice said and Bernie was glad to see a young male security guard there. Clearly they hadn't worried as much about people coming in this way as the main entrance had had proper coppers stationed there.

"That's right, we had to work really hard to sneak out of here earlier," Bernie told him.

"Sneak out?"

"Aye. They wouldn't let my pal here go out front to use her vape, so we had to come out the back."

The security guard snorted. "Ridiculous!"

"I know. And if we don't get back we're going to get a right bollocking from that guy, what's his name again? The really annoying one."

"Steven? The one with the glasses?"

"That's right. Spekkie Steve I call him."

The lad goggled at this insubordination.

"So do you reckon we could scoot in here before we get caught? My pal here's already had two warnings this week. One more and she'll be out."

"Go on then, but you better be quick."

"We will."

Bernie pulled the vaper along behind her and they scurried inside and down a random corridor until they were out of sight.

"I can't believe that worked," Mary said.

"The thing is, most people deep down want to help others when they can. And if you know that then you can use it to your advantage."

"You really are diabolical, aren't you?"

"No need for flattery. Now, which way is the crime scene?"

It took them a few wrong turns in the non-public-facing part of the conference centre to get anywhere interesting. They made their way past an unappealing vista of huge waste bins, abandoned goods' trolleys and stacks of cardboard boxes. Their luck was in, however, as they passed an open maintenance cupboard and managed to grab a couple of hoovers to serve as an alibi.

Mary led them through the main concourse where they pretended to care about the carpet in the café. Bernie took note of where Mary said Tiana had met her for lunch, but it was just an empty table now. Next, they moved towards the main hall, but the police presence was growing thicker. It was only a matter of time until they bumped into someone they knew, but it didn't help that Bernie tripped them up with the hose of her hoover.

DI Macleod did not look impressed.

"Now even I know those are not sci-fi costumes. Just what are you playing at Mrs Paterson?"

Bernie respected the Inspector just enough that she decided the time for bullshit had passed. "We want to help with the case."

"Out of the question. I'll get security to escort you back out of here."

"Come on now," Bernie said, not moving an inch. She could feel Mary cringing in embarrassment next to her, but the fight wasn't over yet. "Mary was actually at the scene. She found the body. Don't you think we have a part to play in this?"

"Yes," Macleod nodded. "Mary does. As a witness. We do not need your PI team skulking around this place."

"I don't skulk," Bernie was affronted. "Mary, have you ever seen me skulk?"

"No. To be fair, that would be a wee bit subtle for you, Berns."

"Exactly. Look, we know that you have about a million interviews to do. The people on stage, the people in the audience, not to mention the members of staff here at the convention. Wouldn't it be a good idea to hire some outside consultants to get you through all the white noise? Some consultants that already have an intimate knowledge of the case."

Macleod's frown flickered for a moment, and Bernie knew she had him.

"I'm not letting you near any suspects."

"Fair enough," Bernie said, then waited while the man chewed his bottom lip.

"But I suppose you could help with the event staff. Only so that we can rule the poor buggers out and send them home. Most of them aren't getting paid for today so they're not in the best of moods."

"We'd be happy to work through them for you."

"All right," Macleod said, giving in with a shrug. "We've already triaged them. You can deal with the people least involved. Take down their details and what they saw and then let them go. Anyone seems in the slightest bit interesting or if they saw our victim at any point in the day, make sure they get passed onto to the constables, okay?"

"Fine," Bernie replied, the grin threatening to break through on her face. "And we'll get our usual rates of course."

"I'll settle it up with finance."

The truth was, they both knew that the WWC were considerably cheaper than pulling in more police officers working on overtime.

"Great," Bernie was flush with triumph. "Just point us in the right direction and we'll get on with it."

"Maybe a change of clothes first?" Macleod pointed at her outfit. "At least lose the hoovers."

"Understood."

Chapter 18: Liz

Liz was experiencing FOMO, which considering she had only recently learned that it meant 'fear of missing out', had come as a bit of a surprise. It was early on Monday morning and instead of attending a WWC meeting, she had received a phone call from Bernie.

"I thought you were coming over today?" Liz had said.

"Changed my mind. I'm in Glasgow with Mary. We're going to see if we can help the police along with this murder at the geek convention."

"Oh I get it," Liz clucked her tongue in frustration. "You're leaving me to deal with this missing parent case while you get to do the fun stuff?"

"I wouldn't call the murder of a young woman fun," Bernie said primly.

"Oh shut up, you're practically buzzing about getting a proper case to look at."

Bernie cackled down the other end of the phone. "I guess you're right. Look at it this way, you can find out more about Linda Novak's case without me moaning about how you should be finding Ryan Porter's dad."

That was true. After Bernie had barked out a few more orders, Liz clicked off the call. She checked her watch and saw that it was nearly twelve. Time to tear Isioma away from the nightmarish cartoon rabbits on the telly and get ready for the nursery session. With any luck she might see Linda there. It would be good to have a conversation with the woman on a more even footing. Liz's eyebrows still stung whenever she touched them. Dave had said they looked very 'new' which she was trying to convince herself was meant to be a compliment.

After the usual fraught moments of trying to get a wriggling two year old into a car seat without losing a) any shoes, socks or hair ties and b) her personal sanity, Liz managed the drive to nursery relatively unscathed. They were the first ones there, and she parked further up the road. She wasn't sure if Linda enjoyed blocking all cars or just of people she thought were killers and it was better to be safe than sorry.

The Renfrewshire weather had settled in early for the day and the rain plopped into the plant pots where someone had tried to plant some flowers months ago. Liz tried not to be too depressed by the dead stalks floating in water. Isioma enjoyed dropping pebbles into them anyway, so that was something.

When it was a half-day session, most of the other kids would already be inside, so Liz rang the bell to go in. It took another interminable length of time to get wellies off, soft shoes on, hair fixed again, lost sock relocated and prepare her beautiful child for entry into the noisy, colourful room that housed two dozen screaming banshees.

"Don't want to go," Isioma had her thumb in her mouth.

"You'll have fun," Liz said, trying not to wince as one child hit another across the back of the head with a picture book.

Isioma didn't look convinced, but she toddled off towards the kitchen area. Liz was just making her way out of the door when she bumped into her quarry.

"Look at what the cat dragged in," Linda sniffed. "Your eyebrows look fabulous by the way. For a con artist."

Liz stiffened. "I explained this already. No one's conning anyone. I'm doing a job for your sister, one that we have been open about from the start. And hopefully we'll be finished soon."

"Sure."

Despite Linda not giving off the 'be my friend' vibe that Liz was hoping for, she moved closer to the other woman.

"I took a quick look at Perrie Mellworth."

"Did you?" Linda kept to a monotone, showing no reaction.

"The police investigated the crash. They didn't find any reason to prosecute. Mellworth was breathalysed at the scene, the road conditions were bad…"

"So you think it was an accident too?" Pink spots had appeared in Linda's cheeks.

"Clearly you don't?"

The other woman was chewing the inside of her cheek. "No."

"Then maybe you should tell me why. I'll even buy you a

coffee."

That got her some eye contact.

"The café down the lane does a decent bacon roll," Linda said slowly, as if her words were betraying her.

"Perfect."

They walked to the café together in silence and found a table in the corner where no one would be able to overhear their conversation. To anyone else, they might have looked like some mum-friends grabbing a cup of tea. Not a potential client and an investigator discussing a suspicious death.

"I don't really know where to start," Linda said. Out of the salon she seemed much more nervous, less sure of herself. "God, I'm probably just being a drama queen. I know that's what Kaylie would think. I should probably just learn to let it go."

"Like Elsa," Liz smiled.

"Aye, my wee ones love that bloody song and all."

The waitress arrived with their coffees and Linda seemed to relax a little now that she had something to do with her hands. Liz watched as she added three brown sugars to the cup and almost grinned at what Bernie would have said about it.

"You don't seem like the sort of person that loves drama," Liz said, wondering if it was true. But she had to get the woman onside somehow.

"No, I'm not. I hate it, actually. I just want to get on with my life and never think about the whole thing ever again. But since that bloody Perrie has started her kid at the nursery I've got to see her every day, like a permanent reminder of the crash. And that day that you saw me, well, I just snapped."

"Did you know him, then?" Liz asked. "The man that died."

"Lenny. Aye, I knew him." Linda blew gently on the foam on top of her latte.

"He was your boyfriend?" Linda gave her a sad smile. "Nope. That's what makes me such a saddo I guess. I was just… we were friends. And I don't believe that the crash was an accident. Perrie must have been drunk, or maybe on something the police don't test for, I don't know. The bit of the road where the crash happened, it's a straight line. No obstacles. Our toddlers could drive it without hitting the barriers."

"I'm sorry, but that doesn't sound like something that will get the police to reopen the case."

"I know. I guess… well, there's probably nothing you can do about it. But I needed someone to talk to, it's not like I could ever mention it to Kaylie."

"Kaylie? What's Kaylie got to do with any of this?"

Another sigh that seemed to come from Linda's feet. "Oh, my perfect sister couldn't let me have him, could she? She knew I fancied Lenny something rotten. But she was the one who asked him out. At the time of the crash they'd just started dating. Six weeks. Not long really. But if you'd seen her at the funeral you'd have thought he was the love of her bloody life. And I... well, I had to sit at the back with all the old women and the folk from his work that hardly knew him. But it was me that was devastated when he died, not her. She shacked up with Ryan a couple of weeks later."

Liz took a long sip of her coffee trying to get her head around this new information.

"So you're telling me that at the time of his death, Kaylie was Lenny's girlfriend?"

"That's right."

"But she wasn't at the party that night?"

Linda sniffed. "She was. But she went home early. She said she was just tired, but who knows? She lies about everything. I always thought maybe she had a fight with Lenny and that's why he went home with that murderous bitch."

An interesting case, that was for sure. They chatted a few minutes longer where Liz brought up the difficult subject of money.

"You understand that we're a paid service, right?"

Linda's eyes dropped. "I don't have much. A couple of hundred quid maybe. And all the free beauty treatments you could handle of course."

Liz knew that Bernie would bite her ear off for working for such a low amount. But she couldn't help but feel sorry for the woman.

"We do sometimes do work at a discount if people can spread the word about our service."

This seemed to cheer the woman up. "Oh, I bet you I can get you loads of clients. Half the woman who come into my work complain that their husband might be cheating on them. And the other half, well, they probably just haven't worked it out yet."

"Excellent," Liz replied. "Then if you can manage a couple of hundred quid I reckon I can sell it to my partners. I've already made a start on the research, and I'll go and speak to Mellworth for you."

"She'll just lie through her teeth," Linda said, her momentary enthusiasm waning.

"That might be true, but our job is to get to the bottom of the lies. I've got some contacts with the local police force and I'll see if I can learn anything about the initial investigation too." Liz didn't mention that her 'contact' was her friend's boyfriend. It sounded more impressive without that little detail.

"But please don't get your hopes up," Liz added. "There's a good chance that Lenny's death was an accident, just like they said at the time."

"Oh I know that woman killed him. She faked the breathalyser or something, I'm sure of it," Linda replied, already grabbing her coat. "I'd just like someone else to believe it too."

Chapter 19: Walker

The hastily set up Major Investigation room didn't have any air conditioning, nevermind windows to open and it was starting to smell of stale sweat and Rav's cheese and onion crisps.

"I was hungry," he said sulkily when Walker suggested that he might have left the packet outside.

"Are you ever not hungry?"

"Sometimes I'm thirsty," Rav replied. "This shift is lasting forever. Do you think they'll ever let us slink off to the pub?"

Walker replied in the negative, although truthfully he wouldn't have minded a couple of hours off himself. The convention centre which had seemed huge when they first came in now felt claustrophobic since they had walked every inch of it. And it didn't help that the case which had been hot was cooling fast. Considering that they had been at the scene when the crime was committed, the lack of suspects was nothing less than embarrassing.

Walker, Rav and the uniformed officers in the room sat up straight as the door banged open and DCI Allan walked in.

"We've got the preliminary findings from the autopsy," she told them, "and I've dragged Professor Ellie Rankin along to talk us through it."

A not-very-happy looking pathologist entered the room,

followed by Macleod who looked like he could do with a good sleep. Walker was pleased to see Rankin, even if she didn't seem quite so happy to be there. The Professor was young and ambitious and Walker had never seen her be anything other than a hundred per cent thorough in her work. She could be harsh if she felt someone hadn't done their homework, but her expertise was clear to see.

"I still reckon we could have done this over the phone," the pathologist said as she plugged in her laptop. "I have been up since five to do the PM."

"This is a significant investigation," the DCI said, shooting the other woman daggers. "With a lot of media attention."

The Professor just shrugged and Walker was impressed she wasn't about to let herself be intimidated by the DCI.

"All right, let me bring up the files here," Rankin said, squinting at the screen. A projector had been found from somewhere and a slightly flickery image appeared on the wall. "I've uploaded everything to HOLMES, but I guess I can go through each of the results, if that's what you're after."

A nod from the DCI showed her assent.

"All right. Let's start with an overview. The victim was identified as Tiana Schmidt, a US citizen who was currently resident in London. Now, the identification has not been confirmed yet as her mother is flying over from America, so we've had to technically mark that as a provisional ID, although I guess you're pretty certain."

"Yes, her colleagues positively identified her."

"Good," the Professor did a curt nod. "We have a female in her early thirties in well-nourished condition. No obvious abnormalities with the body. One wound site on the back of the head."

"Was that the cause of death?" the DCI barked.

Rankin glared at her and carried on as if no one had interrupted. "I conducted the autopsy with two assistants at eight this morning. I'm going to summarize the findings for you, but you can view the full report yourself and feedback any questions. Now, as I said, these are the findings of the preliminary examination. Toxicology results won't be back today, maybe tomorrow if you're lucky."

The Professor then went into a long and frankly dull discussion about the autopsy. Complete with images of the dissection that were not for the squeamish. From what Walker could tell, it seemed like Tiana Schmidt had been the picture of health, until she wasn't.

"So to sum up, no abnormalities in any of the major organs, no damage to heart or liver. The only sign of injury is in the cranial region."

The tension in the room went up a notch.

"Here is a picture of the wound before we cleaned it up."

Walker was interested to see that barely any blood was visible. He had been beating himself up for not spotting the wound at the crime scene, but actually there wasn't much to see.

"Why so little blood?" Macleod asked.

"Good question," the pathologist said, earning her a smile from the DI and a glare from Allen. "I've looked at the pictures of the crime scene and it does seem like there's an unusually small amount of blood."

"Could she have been killed elsewhere?"

"Possible, but unlikely," Walker answered. "We walked the area yesterday. You would have to go past so many people carrying a body, it just doesn't seem likely that anyone could have done it elsewhere and brought her there without being caught."

"There are a couple of medical explanations," the pathologist said. "One could be that the wound was inflicted post mortem."

"But that would mean there was another cause of death," the DCI frowned.

"Yes, and we haven't found evidence of that. But we still need to consider it as a possibility. Another possible reason is the skull fracture itself. Sometimes the wound can occur in a way that the swelling of the soft tissue seals up the fracture."

"All right," the DCI made a note on her pad, "let's assume for now that's the case. Any ideas on the murder weapon?"

"All we can say is that the point of impact was at least three inches across. So nothing sharp. But it might be something that she was hit with, or pushed into."

Macleod brought up the pictures of the damaged lighting rig on his tablet. "Is there anything here on the rig that might have caused the injury? In which case it could have been an accident."

But the Professor was already shaking her head. "I don't believe so. I'll take some more time to examine it in depth, of course, but if the positions of the corpse and the lighting rig in the photos are accurate, I can't see any part that might have injured her. You're looking at something rectangular, with smooth edges."

The faces in the room suggested that this wasn't the great breakthrough that the police officers were hoping for.

"Sorry to be the bearer of bad news," Professor Rankin said. "But you're going to have to put the miles in on this one. Call me when you've got a potential murder weapon and I might be able to match it to the skull fractures." Even this didn't sound particularly hopeful.

"One more thing, Professor," the DCI held up her hand. "We could really do with a definitive time of death."

"You know it's not an exact science, right?" The Professor tutted. "But the police officers at the scene noted that the remains were already cold and rigor had started to set in. When we took the probes back at the morgue, it gave us an estimated time of death around one to two o'clock in the afternoon."

This was significant, Walker thought.

"It means that she was most likely dead long before the lighting platform fell," Rav said, articulating what they were all thinking. It also meant that the alibi of being on the panel was no alibi at all.

"On the balance of probability, yes." Professor Rankin closed down her laptop and left the room muttering something about finally getting some coffee. The DCI's face looked like she'd just seen a storm cloud coming down over her washing line.

"Well that was a waste of bloody time," Allan moaned. "Please tell me that you've got something better for me on the interviews today."

There were a few raised eyebrows around the room. It was rare for a senior officer to criticise a pathologist like that. Walker wondered just how much pressure Allan was on from the media and her superiors. He was glad in that moment that he was a lowly sergeant.

"We're working on them, sir," Walker said in reply to her question.

"Suspects?"

Walker noticed Macleod's shoulders slump.

"Few on the ground. We'll be getting the head technician from the conference centre back in for a second interview. He was responsible for the lighting rig that collapsed. But so far we've got nothing."

"Any connection to our mysterious letter writer?"

"If there is, it's not an obvious one. We're going to look through Tiana's phone, but from what we can tell she wasn't targeted by our letter writer."

"It's a coincidence, then?"

"Could be," Macleod admitted. "But I think it's still worth looking into the letter writer. Someone who wishes harm on others and goes to the extent of turning up at their hotel room, well that seems to me like the sort of risk taker that would kill a woman in the middle of a convention."

"I agree," the DCI said. "Let's keep both investigations running in parallel. Although the overtime is going to mount up and I'm not sure how I'll justify it to the Superintendent if we don't get some better leads soon."

"I've brought in some consultants," Macleod said, clearing his throat. "They know the event well so I've put them to work on some preliminary enquiries. Should free our guys up to do the hard work."

Luckily, Allan seemed distracted by some messages coming in on her phone so she didn't remark on the new consultants. Walker knew full well who that would be. He just had to hope that the ladies of the WWC didn't bring too much attention on themselves. For once.

Chapter 20: Mary

Mary Plunkett was still not quite sure how Bernie had not only got them into the convention centre but even got them official status within the investigation. But she was very much enjoying her 'police visitor pass' lanyard which was almost as nice as her convention one. Less rainbows, but still nice.

So far, however, she didn't feel like she had added much to the investigation. Two cleaners and a barista from the café had come over to give statements, but none of them had seen Tiana before she died. Bernie was interviewing people at the other end of the conference room, but judging from the woman's pursed lips and tight shoulders, she wasn't getting on any better.

Time for a break, Mary thought, getting up and making her way over to the cubicle in the wall that was the closest place to get a cuppa.

"Got any pastries or anything?" Mary asked the woman behind the counter who poured her some grey-looking tea out of an urn. She was in her sixties with short black hair and a massive bosom that Mary worried was going to knock the milk over.

"I've got a sad almond croissant but it's three quid," the woman said, her apology sounding all the more morose due to the low tones of her Fife accent.

"It'll do, thanks. Got to keep my strength up." Mary took the stale-looking plastic-wrapped croissant and popped it into her handbag.

"You with the police?"

"Sort of. I'm a private investigator but we're helping out with the interviews. They've got hundreds of people to get through."

"It's a bloody nightmare. That poor woman. Word is someone bashed her over the head."

Yet again, Mary was impressed by the power of gossip.

"I don't think the police know for sure yet," she said vaguely. "We're just trying to interview as many people as possible so we can find out what happened to her."

"Probably some junkie nutter trying to rob her. Poor lass. She popped in here and all. Can't have been long before she died."

Mary turned back to the stall. "She did?"

"Aye. I noticed her because she had a funny accent."

"Transatlantic," Mary agreed. "Kind of a mix between American and English."

"That's right. We got to chatting for a bit. She wanted to try the shortbread. It's not bad actually, and only two quid."

"What time was this?"

"Well, let's see, I'd just had my second break, so around quarter past four."

Mary's heart quickened. This was after her own meeting with Schmidt and less than half an hour before she had discovered her body.

"How did she seem? Did you think she was worried about anything?"

The other woman shook her head. "Naw, she was relaxed. Sort of slow-talking in that American way, you know? Like I said, she was just chatting about shortbread. And then this prick in a suit came over and pulled her away."

"Really?"

"Yeah. I guess he was her boss or something. He said the panel was starting soon and she was needed to fix their make-up. I hadn't even realised before that that she was a make-up woman."

"Was the guy kind of thin?"

"Aye, with one of those silly little beards that men should just shave off."

Mary nodded. The description fitted Tony Ashley, and he sounded like the sort of man who would enjoy throwing his weight around.

"He was angry with her, is that right?"

Realisation seemed to dawn on the other woman's face. "Well, not 'I'm going to kill someone angry'. Just like a boss who wasn't very good at keeping his temper. Like when Barry who runs the food concessions starts moaning about people going out for a ciggie. Just wanting to make himself sound important."

Still, it was worth noting. Mary took down the woman's name – Marianne Edwards – and told her that the police would want to talk to her.

"They'll have to buy a coffee," Marianne said with a sniff. "I'm not allowed any more breaks."

"I'm sure that will be fine."

Mary made her way back to the conference room feeling a little lighter. At least she had something she could share with Macleod to prove that the WWC were worth the money. She was feeling pretty happy with herself right up until she bit into the croissant. Marianne had been right. It was not worth three quid.

Chapter 21: Bernie

It had become clear to Bernie quite early on that she had been assigned the most menial of the interviews when it came to the death of Tiana Schmidt. Despite what she had said to Macleod, she was not happy with the dregs of the Police Scotland case.

In this mood, she decided to reward herself with a nice lunch. She could have invited Mary to come along, but she had spied the younger woman munching her way through a croissant and didn't want to encourage any more over-indulgence.

"I'm just popping out for food," she told the uniformed constable guarding the entrance to the investigation room. It took her a few minutes to work out where the main entrance to the convention was, given that she had snuck in the back earlier, but soon she was out into the bracing September wind.

She checked the information on her phone. Sure enough, the tall ugly building across the road which was all windows and steel was the convention hotel. The imaginatively named 'Convention Plaza' looked like any mid-range hotel you might find in any country in the world. Mary would have found it soulless, but Bernie was inclined to approve of the utilitarian nature of these sorts of places. It did exactly what you expected, nothing less and certainly nothing more.

"How can I be of assistance?" A round-looking man with a receding hairline and a Glasgow accent greeted her at the reception desk.

"I've got a few questions," Bernie said. She held up the police visitor pass that she had carefully forgotten to hand back to the gormless constable on her way out.

"Oh, I thought we were finished with all that. The deputy manager, Gloria, spoke to one of your lot the other day about the letters."

Ah yes, the threatening letters. In all the excitement of investigating the death of Tiana Schmidt, Bernie had forgotten that the reason for the police presence in the first place had been some nasty notes.

"It's actually some of your residents that I would like to speak to. I believe that you have some members of the *Vampyra* cast staying here?"

"That's right. Most of them were meant to leave today but your lot have asked them to stay on for a few days. Played havoc with our reservations."

Bernie didn't feel much sympathy. "I was wondering if you could call some of them down from their rooms for me. It would just be a quick chat."

The receptionist was starting to look uncomfortable. "Well, I'm not sure how many of them are actually in their rooms at the moment. We're not running a prison after all."

"Décor's kind of similar though, right?"

The man blinked. "Sorry, what did you say?"

"Look, are any of the members of the *Vampyra* cast or crew in their rooms? I have a list of names here. If you find someone for me then I'll be out of your hair in a few minutes."

The attraction of this idea proved too much for the Receptionist.

"As a matter of fact, I saw Miss Strong go upstairs a short while ago. I could call her room and see if she might be available."

Bernie watched as the man keyed the number into the phone on the desk. After a few moments of muttered conversation, he replaced the handset.

"I'm afraid Miss Strong says she is expecting an important phone call at the moment. She will be available after lunch."

"Fair enough," Bernie shrugged. "Can I use your loo before I go?"

"There are guest toilets in the restaurant," the man said, managing a smile now that Bernie seemed to be playing nicely. Of course, if he had known her even slightly then he would understand that Bernie Paterson never gave up on anything.

The restaurant was down a long corridor but once she was out of sight of the front desk, Bernie took a left instead to the lifts. It only took a few minutes for her to get to the twelfth floor and find room number 1283. If the Receptionist hadn't wanted her to come upstairs to Anetta Strong's room then they should have a better telephone system than just hitting nine and entering the room number.

Bernie rapped on the door a few times until it opened. An extraordinarily beautiful face confronted her, even though it was set in a frown.

"It's Bernie Paterson," she said, holding her police visitors pass up for inspection. "I called up about an interview."

"I'm afraid I'm busy at the moment. I did tell the Receptionist that."

"Did you? How strange. He said to just go on up. Well, seeing as I'm here, I don't suppose you could spare me five minutes of your time. I won't be any trouble." Bernie gave the actress her sweetest smile, which made the woman move back a pace, just enough for Bernie to get her toe in the door.

"Five minutes then," Anetta said finally and she went back into the room.

It was a nice suite, with a sofa and table in front of the large windows and the bed area largely out of sight behind a stud wall. Bernie had a quick look for murder weapons or signed confessions, but sadly there were none of those lying around. Instead, there was a pile of papers on the table that looked like they might be scripts and a few items of clothing that probably cost more than Bernie's car flung over chairs.

"*My Right Eye?*" Bernie read out the name on one of the scripts. "What's that, the sequel to *My Left Foot?*"

"Hardly," Anetta snapped and she picked up the papers and shoved them into a handbag. "You don't seem much like a police officer."

"I'm a consultant," Bernie explained. "Plus, police are kind of different in this country. They don't go around shooting people, for one thing."

Anetta picked at her nail. "Look, my management company said any more involvement with the police and I had to get a lawyer."

"Oh yeah, you should definitely do that. As soon as they caution you, you start yelling for a lawyer. I can tell you're smart. But like I said, I'm just a consultant. And we're just having a cosy chat, right?"

The other woman crossed her arms. "Let's just get on with it."

Bernie pulled out a notepad, but it was just for show. She had already set her mobile to record in her pocket but people got angsty if she mentioned that and she hated when suspects went on about their human rights.

"You don't seem too upset about Tiana's death," Bernie said. "I mean, you don't look like you've been crying or anything."

"What are you, the emotion police?" Anetta didn't look to offended. In fact, she didn't look too bothered in general. One of those people who were easily bored, Bernie thought. And not too bright either, which was always a plus for the interviewer.

"I suppose I just wondered how well you knew the woman."

"As well as you get to know anyone on a TV set. I mean, it's not as glamorous as it looks. Most of the time I just turn up and say my lines then go home, you know?"

Bernie didn't really, but she nodded as if she did. "But you must have spent quite a lot of time in make-up. It's a show about dragons and stuff, isn't it?"

"Yeah, but I'm a vampire, not a dragon. So it's just pale make-up and smoky eyes. It only took Tiana fifteen minutes or so. Not like with someone like Stefan who had those ridiculous elf-ears to put on."

"Right," Bernie was floundering a bit now. What kind of show had vampires and dragons and elves? The crash course Mary had given her in the *Vampyra* world clearly hadn't been thorough enough. "So you weren't close to Tiana?"

"Like I said, we were both professionals. We made small talk, sometimes she would talk about her dog, I have a cat… nothing more than that."

"What about anyone else? Who was she friends with on the set?"

"Well, she was rumoured to be one of Stefan's conquests, but I reckon that's bullshit. He definitely liked them younger and prettier. And I think she sometimes hung around with the writers, although god knows why. Not a deodorant between the lot of them if you get my meaning."

Bernie did. "Was there anyone she might have fallen out with? Did anyone have a reason to hurt her?"

"I wouldn't have thought so. In fact, I would think it's quite obvious that Tiana was just collateral damage."

"What does that mean?"

Another sigh. "I told the police about those letters. They should have done something about it, but they didn't give a crap. And now Tiana is dead."

"You think whoever wrote the threatening letters killed her?"

"Of course. Some psycho that hated the show. And hated women. Are you trying to tell me there aren't plenty of those around?"

Bernie couldn't exactly argue that point. But she wasn't so sure that the sort of creep who wrote nasty anonymous letters would be bold enough to bash a woman over the head in a public place.

"Do you have any idea of anyone else who might have had it in for Tiana?" Bernie asked her, aware that time was running out. She wasn't expecting an answer, but the other woman hesitated.

"No."

"You were going to say something there."

Anetta pouted. "I don't have any proof, and I know how much you police types love proof."

"Like I told you, I'm not police."

"All right then. You need to talk to Gigorath," Anetta said. "If I were you, I'd be taking a good look at that old freak. How he had the nerve to show up today, I'll never know."

"Giga what?"

"His name is Fletcher Moon, he played Gigorath in the show. Hammed it up like nothing on earth, but the fans loved him for some reason. I swear, every scene I was in he forced himself into the best light. Absolute idiot."

"All right, he sounds like a dick," Bernie admitted, "but why should I ask him about Tiana?"

"Because she got him fired, didn't she? It's an open secret on the set. The writers were pissed because they had to squeeze in a death scene for him before the end of the season. He was meant to be a recurring character, but the stupid a-hole couldn't keep his hands to himself."

"He was inappropriate with Tiana?"

"Must have been. Why else would she have got him sacked?"

Bernie tried to pick this further with Anetta, but the woman didn't seem to know any details, only the vaguest rumours that she had heard on set. If the conversation wasn't about herself, Miss Strong seemed to lose interest pretty quickly. When her phone rang, Anetta pointed Bernie towards the door and she was happy to leave.

It turned out that Bernie found actresses kind of irritating, and unlike Mary she didn't give two craps about the dragon show. But at least Anetta had given her a couple of leads. Now she just had to decide what to share with the cops and what to keep all for herself.

Chapter 22: Liz

While Bernie and Mary were living their best lives dealing with a murder inquiry in Glasgow, Liz was getting lower back pain from being hunched over her laptop all day. No matter what she tried or where she looked, there seemed to be no sign of Marty Gortat. It was looking more and more likely that Gortat wasn't even his real name. She had asked Mary if Walker could take a look and see if the man had a police record, but even if he wanted to help, they were far too busy with the murder of Tiana Schmidt. No one from the Renfrewshire Polish group had got back to her yet and she was running low on options.

And there was the temptation of the allegations that Linda had made about the car crash. They had no relation to the Kaylie/Ryan wedding, but Liz found herself constantly wishing she was investigating that case instead.

She let out a low groan when another 'M Gortat' on social media turned out to be the wrong age for her quarry.

"Something the matter?" Dave poked his head around the door. He had started a new partner in his Optician's business a month ago so that he had more time at home. If Liz was honest, she was finding his constant presence in her formerly quiet house more than a little irritating.

"Just a work thing being a nightmare."

He came over and perched on the arm of the sofa. "Would it help if you talked it through with me?"

Liz raised an eyebrow. "You don't normally ask about my cases."

"Because you don't normally look so defeated," Dave said. "I mean, since you quit your old job, it's like you can't wait to get to your laptop. I've never seen you so excited about something as when you joined the WWC. So it's kind of unusual to see you sighing and moping around."

For Dave, who wasn't the most emotional of men, this was quite a long speech, so Liz sat up and considered her reply.

"It's not even really a case," she explained. "Just a personal obsession of someone connected to another case. And I should be spending my time on the one that we're actually getting paid for."

"But this other problem is on your mind?"

She nodded. "If Linda Novak is correct then someone has got away with murder."

"And you can't just let that go?"

Liz's mouth turned down at the corners. "Do you think I should?"

Her husband bent down and gave her an awkward hug. "No. Look, I know sometimes I drive you crazy because I don't plan things, or I don't worry about the future, or think about the big questions, all that stuff."

"It doesn't drive me crazy," Liz lied.

Dave chuckled. "Sure. But the reason I don't worry about any of that stuff is because I know that you'll take care of it. And maybe that makes me a weak beta male or something, but that's the way it is. I trust your judgement and I know that you'll make the right decision, no matter what the circumstances are."

A warm glow spread through her chest. "So I should trust my instincts?"

"Exactly."

"Thanks."

Dave wandered off to the kitchen where he would no doubt make a sandwich directly on the worktop and not clean up the crumbs. But maybe that didn't matter too much if he was willing to support her like he just had. Liz breathed out and opened a new file. She saved it as 'Perrie Mellworth crash'.

When Linda Novak had first flagged up the case, Liz had skim-read the brief articles online about the car crash. It had happened in October 2022. Late at night on a Friday, a car driven by Perrie Mellworth had crashed into the barrier on the motorway. It had been pouring rain, conditions were bad and no fault was found with the driver. The passenger had been killed instantly.

The passenger's name was Lenny Ingot, and this was the lad that Linda had loved but that Kaylie had taken away from her. Some of the internet sites had his picture. A man in his mid-twenties who looked five years younger in the photos where he was wearing a polo shirt with a shock of curly hair that fell over one eye. Liz checked if he still had any social media pages up. There was one, with an RIP post featuring photos clearly put up by his mum as they started with baby pics right up to the present day. As a fellow mother, Liz felt a pang of sympathy. There was nothing worse than having your child die before you.

She took a deep breath and scanned through the RIP comments. There were hundreds of them, but none from Linda or Kaylie for that matter. Mind you, they might have sent private messages instead, it was hard to tell.

Instead, Liz had a look through Kaylie's personal pictures. There were thousands of the bloody things. It was easy to get judgemental after the hundredth duck-pout pose, but Liz knew that it was just as unlikely that people who posted these things were insecure as they were vain. Eventually, she managed to scroll back to October 2022

There were a couple of photos of Kaylie and Lenny, but not that many, proof that what Linda had said about them only going out for a few weeks was true. And then a day after the crash there was just a broken-hearted emoji. That was all the acknowledgement from Kaylie that her boyfriend had been killed. Interesting.

It was all very tragic, but Liz wasn't sure there was a case here. Perrie Mellworth had been breathalysed at the scene, so it wasn't like she was drunk behind the wheel. Still, she was probably worth a quick look. Liz stretched out her back and returned to the laptop.

But to Liz's chagrin, Mellworth didn't have any social media.

How irritating. Not that Liz had any herself, of course, she was far too cognisant of how other people could use the information, seeing as it was her job to do just that. What was Mellworth's reason for evading prying eyes?

There was nothing for it, Liz would have to visit the woman in person. A bit of digging found that a Peregrina Mellworth worked for a local delivery firm in the main office. The address was easy enough to find, and after making sure Dave was happy to watch Isioma, she headed off to the centre of Invergryff.

The delivery firm was in an old warehouse that still had the faded remnants of the previous business's sign over the door. This firm had the uninspiring name of Allied Solutions Ltd, with half a dozen plain white vans outside. Liz pulled into a spare space and hoped that no one would give her a ticket for being in a 'strictly employees only' spot.

Luckily for Liz, Perrie Mellworth was sitting right in front of her when she opened the door. It was easy enough to recognise her, mainly because she had a nametag with 'Perrie' over her right breast. The woman looked younger than her twenty-five years, the sort of person who would get ID'd for alcohol until she was thirty. Tiny, with a long thin face and big dark eyes, she already looked nervous before Liz had even spoken.

"Perrie Mellworth? My name's Liz. I'd like to have a quick word with you."

"It's not about that delivery to the sawmill, is it? I'm really sorry I got the postcode the wrong way around but I didn't realise until the big rig was on its way and —"

Liz had to hold her hand up to get the woman to stop. "No, it's nothing about work."

"Oh good," Perrie managed a weak smile. "Only I'm on my last warning."

An over-sharer who liked to talk, Liz thought. Sometimes her job was a little too easy.

"It's something personal. Is there anywhere we can go to talk."

The woman's eyes bulged wide. "No... I mean, there's the staff room, but my boss is in there."

"All right. We can do it here if you like. I wanted to ask you about the death of Lenny Ingot."

Perrie reacted as if Liz had slapped her. "I don't... that was an accident. I don't like to talk about it."

"I'm afraid you might have to," Liz said sternly. There was something about Perrie's wide-eyed nervousness that brought out her tough side.

"But the police said the case was closed. And I... well, I'm not talking about it anymore. It's not good for my mental health."

Perhaps on a different day, Liz might have sympathised. But she had just spent an hour looking at Lenny's mother's grief-stricken posts about her dead son.

"I'm actually here to help. You see, we were notified that there might be some harassment going on, and we just wanted to check in with you." Liz was slightly horrified at how easily the lie came to her lips. But all was fair in the pursuit of a killer.

"Harassment?"

"People posting stuff online. You know, that it wasn't an accident after all."

The girl winced once more. "But everyone knows it was an accident. No one meant to kill Lenny, the car just slipped. It was no one's fault."

"You were the driver, but it wasn't your fault?"

"No! I wasn't... it was an accident. Just like the police said. And I'm not sure what you mean about harassment. No one's been saying anything to me online."

"That might be because you deleted all your social media, didn't you? I checked and you used to have the usual profiles, but after the crash you got rid of them all."

"I needed a break," she sniffed. "Look, I'm meant to be working right now. I think you should leave, or I'll call my boss."

Liz left the woman practically wobbling off her seat with stress. She could have kept pushing Mellworth, but she reckoned it was better to sow the first seeds of doubt in the woman's mind. And besides, Liz had already learned that the case was worth investigating. In four years of being in the WWC Liz had never met anyone before who was so clearly lying. Now she just had to find out why.

Chapter 23: Walker

Walker had no idea how Bernie and Mary had talked their way into the briefing room, but there they were, standing at the back, looking like they owned the place. Bernie gave him a smug nod and Mary a cheery wave so that Walker had to hide the smile that crept across his face.

"Don't," Macleod said when he saw his expression. "Just don't, okay? Sometimes you've got to make a deal with the devil."

He was about to press the DI for details when the door opened and DCI Allan entered. Although Macleod was technically the SIO on this case, the mere fact that Allan was around to deal with the media attention meant that the briefing had defaulted to her.

If Allan had spotted the WWC members, she wisely decided to ignore them and without any preamble went straight into the business of the day.

"All right everyone. Now we're coming to the end of the day shift, but I'm afraid we've still plenty of work to do. I've just had the finished profile come in on our victim. Her identity has now been positively confirmed as Tiana Schmidt, age thirty-four. US citizen, born in New Jersey. Professional make-up artist working on TV sets, which is why she was here at the convention. She was part of the cast and crew members of a show called *Vampyra*, which is apparently a popular fantasy-type series."

Walker knew Mary would be raging at the disdainful way the DCI had said 'fantasy'.

"As you should all already be aware, the members of the cast were already part of a police investigation as there had been threatening letters left at two cast members' hotel rooms. DI Macleod here was conducting an investigation into these messages when Ms Schmidt was killed. One possible line of inquiry, therefore, is that our letter writer struck out, but not at the people we were expecting he would."

"Another item of relevance to the investigation is the sabotage of the lighting rig. Now, initially we thought that might have been responsible for Tiana's death, seeing as she was discovered just after it went down. However, the pathologist has confirmed that Tiana was most likely dead before this occurrence, and this is in accordance with officer reports from the scene. The remains were already cold by the time the rig went down."

There was a murmur of irritation in the room. Every officer there could tell this case was going to be a nightmare.

DCI Allan raised her voice. "I know this is a difficult one. It's going to be a case of getting through the numbers. We need to get through every single witness statement as quickly as possible. DI Macleod is going to look into Miss Schmidt's personal life. We've just got her phone access from tech so we're hoping there might be something on it to give us a clue to her killer. Check your actions for me and if you're not assigned to anything in particular, you're taking statements.

Let's get this done as quickly as possible."

Walker checked his watch. He was due off-duty soon, but he didn't feel like going anywhere. This was the sort of policing he loved: right in the thick of an investigation when any lead could change the entire case.

"I've got something for you," Mary said, appearing at his side. She explained about the chat that she'd had with Marianne at the coffee kiosk.

"Bernie looked up the official statements," Mary told him. "And it seems that Tony Ashley didn't mention that he'd spoken to Tiana not long before she died."

"That is interesting," Walker replied. "Ashley? He's part of the crew, right?"

"He's the producer. He was on the panel on Saturday."

Walker rubbed at his stubble. "So he would be Tiana's boss, right?"

"Right."

Worth following up for sure, Walker thought. "I'll tell Macleod right now," he said.

"At least I'm earning my keep," Mary smiled at him. "Between Tony Ashley and that forum chat I sent you, that's got to count as a couple of good leads."

"What forum chat?"

"The one where people were threatening Anetta. I emailed

you it the other day."

Walker was puzzled. "I'm pretty sure I never got it."

"I definitely sent it," Mary replied, the tiny frown line appearing between her eyebrows like it always did when she was annoyed. "Let me check. Yeah, I sent you an email on Sunday morning, before Tiana was killed."

Walker pulled out his own phone. "All right, let's see. Okay, you sent me an email with check-out this link, and then when I clicked it was a website that sold Christmas outfits for cats. I was kind of confused as it was a) September and b) we don't own a cat. But I just thought it was one of your jokes that I don't always get."

"Oh crap, I meant to send that one to Bernie to annoy her. For some weird reason she refuses to dress up her cat at all. Can you imagine?"

"Could we focus on the possible vital evidence at this point, please," Walker said, placing his hand on her arm to lessen how snippy he sounded.

"Of course. I'm resending it. But here, you can have a look on my phone anyway."

He took it from her and scrolled down through the thread on the forum. Just as Mary had said, it seemed more targeted than the usual nasty internet trolling.

"I'll pass it on to the tech specialists. Maybe they can link one of these guys with the ones sending threatening DMs to Anetta."

"Do you think that whoever killed Tiana was trying to get Anetta somehow and it went wrong? A mistaken identity type thing?" Mary asked.

Walker shook his head slowly. "I've talked about it with Macleod, but I don't see how. Tiana was short, curvy, nothing like Anetta. They were dressed differently too, so even from the back, I don't see how you could confuse them."

"I don't either."

"But that doesn't mean Anetta wasn't the real target. Maybe Tiana confronted the person who was rigging the lighting platform to fall. Her death was just a way of keeping it quiet."

"That sounds more likely," Mary said, shuffling from one foot to the other. "It didn't seem like a pre-planned murder. I mean, who would choose to kill someone there. It was just luck that no one walked in on them when it was happening."

"If the blow from behind killed her, like we're assuming, she never even had a chance to cry out," Walker said, watching the other officers file out of the room to take statements. It wasn't until he turned back to his girlfriend that he realised she was crying.

"Hey, it's okay," he said, pulling Mary into his arms for a quick hug.

"God, I'm sorry. I should be used to this. It's not like it's my first murder or anything. It's not even my first dead body. But I was talking to her, and now she's gone and all because she got in the way of some psycho trying to do bad stuff to other people."

Walker brushed a lock of hair out of her eyes. "I know. And I'd love to tell you it's all for a reason, and that justice will be served and all that crap. But sometimes life just sucks. We can only do our best with what we have. And right now our best is finding who hurt Tiana and making sure they never have the chance to do it to someone else."

He pulled away from her, remembering that he was meant to be at work, not cuddling with his girlfriend. As he looked away he caught Rav's eye who gave him a smirk.

"I better go and find Macleod," Walker said, stepping away from Mary. "You know that if I didn't have to do my job I would take you home, pour you a bath and put on ABBA's greatest hits for you."

"Charmer," Mary said, and Walker was relieved to see her smiling again.

"I try," he said. "Are you sticking around or heading off?"

"Heading home I think. We've been here since first thing this morning and Bernie's moaning about missing her spin class. Besides, the kids get back from camping tonight and I'm dying to catch up with them. See you tomorrow?"

"Sure," Walker said, although he knew he couldn't promise anything. It was a murder case so anything could change at any moment. He just had to hope that Mary would understand that.

Macleod came back into the room just as Mary was leaving.

"I'm going to speak to the forensics guys, want to come? I've dragged them out of the lab to talk us through the scene."

You could tell this was a case in the public eye, Walker thought as he saw the team of forensic specialists standing in the cordoned-off area where Tiana had been found. Of course, any murder inquiry would have had a specialist forensic team, but that was normally a Crime Scene Manager and maybe one other person. There were six people here jostling for space, and when Walker and Macleod joined them it was more than a little cosy.

"Let's get this done quickly so we can get out of this sweatbox," Macleod told them. "I understand that you've sent over your reports, but I want you to talk us through the scene and tell us what you found."

The man that stepped forward introduced himself as Rob Enright and he had the sort of milky skin that you got from working all hours in a laboratory. "All right. Well, as you already know we've had a bit of a struggle with this one. Plenty of trace evidence, but it being such a public place, it's been tricky to tell what formed part of the crime and what was just extraneous matter. So we focused on the area immediately around Miss Schmidt's remains. We found several hairs and fibres underneath her body, but you're going to have a hard time proving they were left by any particular subject."

Macleod let out a groan at this news and the forensics guys gave him sympathetic looks.

"It's a problem of transference," Enright explained. "So many people were in and out of this area that it's going to be near to impossible to prove when the evidence was deposited. We can't look at a hair sample or a fingerprint and say for definite that it was left there at the time of the murder. Not unless it was left in a pool of blood or something."

Macleod's dour face showed what he felt about that. "I don't suppose you've got a fingerprint left in blood for me then?"

"Afraid not. But I have managed to find something on the lighting rig."

The man led them through the heavy curtain to the stage. The rig itself had been removed to the lab, but Enright had come armed with some printouts.

"We looked over every inch of this thing. We now know how it was brought down. Simple enough really. They just loosened a couple of bolts on one side. As soon as the lights started moving that was just enough vibration to tip it over."

"Would you need to be a professional to do it?"

The technician shook his head. "No. Anyone could have done it. But it was risky. It could have come down in ten minutes or an hour."

Macleod frowned as he thought this through. "All right. What have you got for me?"

"If you look at the pictures, the print was found on the underside here, not somewhere you would just brush against when passing by. And it's left in grease. This grease is an exact match to the stuff on the hinges where the loose bolts were. We know from the elimination prints that it doesn't match any of the lighting engineers here, so we might just have got lucky."

"You've already checked the fingerprint for known matches?"

"Yes. It's not in the system. But if you can find a match with a suspect you might just have something that would stand up in court."

"Great. We just need a bloody suspect now."

Noticing that the CSM's face had fallen, Macleod clapped him on the back. "You've done good work here, better than I was hoping for. It's not your fault this case is a fecking nightmare."

"Let's run that print against all the elimination ones we took from the *Vampyra* cast to start with," Macleod said. "I don't suppose you found the same print anywhere near Tiana's body?"

"Afraid not," Enright replied. "I'll be in touch if we find anything else."

Macleod glowered at the technicians as they shuffled back out of the room, leaving them alone.

"Type this all up for the report will you?" Macleod asked Walker who nodded. "I've put Sergeant Sangar on the CCTV footage. Maybe he's found something by now."

But when they got to the security room they found a fed-up looking Rav with two uniformed officers staring at some grainy video.

"It's a nightmare, sir," Rav told Macleod as soon as they walked in. "There's plenty of CCTV on the exits and entrances, plus around the food stalls, but barely anything in the main hall. We're going to keep looking, but I can't see that it's going to be much use."

Walker didn't need to see Macleod's face to know how that news would go down.

"Let's go back over the interviews," Macleod said. "Someone has got to have seen something."

Rav met Walker's eyes and gave him a small shrug. There was only so much they could do if there wasn't any evidence. Walker found himself hoping that the WWC might manage to come up with something. He would even settle for putting up with Bernie's smug expression if she found something to break the case open. At the moment, they were just staggering around in the dark.

Chapter 24: Mary

Mary had woken up on Tuesday morning feeling tired in her bones. She had only made it back from Glasgow five minutes before Matt and Stephanie turned up with the kids the night before. It had been time to plaster on the mum smile.

Thankfully, it never took long for the fake smile to turn into a real one. This time her grin widened when she saw Stephanie gingerly carrying a Tupperware tub like it looked like it was about to explode.

"Let me guess, Gary escaped?" Mary said, taking pity on the poor woman and removing the tub from her outstretched hands. Was it a little petty that Mary was enjoying the smudged mascara on the woman's cheeks and the tiny twigs in her normally immaculate bun?

"His jar smashed somehow when we were putting up the tent," Stephanie said, in the sort of voice normally only heard from hurricane survivors. "We spent two hours looking for him. We'd just given up hope when guess whose maccha tea he was sitting in, having a wee bath."

"Oh god, I'm sorry."

"No, it's fine. And the kids are great really," she glanced at Matt who was corralling the children and rucksacks toward the house. "I shouldn't complain. We had a lovely time."

For a second, Mary wanted to put her arm around the woman,

but it was just too awkward. She settled for giving Stephanie's hand a quick squeeze. "Honestly, it's okay. Holidays with the kids are always ninety per cent lovely and ten per cent total car wreck. If the worst that happened was a lost stick insect, you've done great."

"Thanks," Stephanie said.

Matt reappeared. "They've already got the telly on so they must have had enough of the outdoors."

"Of course. See you in a few days?"

"Sure," he said, getting into the driver's seat as quickly as he could. Maybe it wasn't just Stephanie that hadn't found the weekend all marshmallows and joyful campfire songs.

"Oh, and Gary might have to be renamed," Stephanie called out to Mary as they started to drive away. "Maybe Gloria instead? Take a look in the box."

With the sort of dread that anyone who had watched the movie Se7en would understand, Mary opened the box. There was the now inappropriately named Gary, with a dozen little mini Garys crawling all over the place.

Stephanie gave her a cheery wave as the car drove off. Mary resisted the urge to return a less appropriate hand gesture. The new woman had definitely won this round.

By the next morning, Mary had just about managed to get her equilibrium back. Garyetta and her babies had been moved into an old hamster cage with some leaves to keep them going. Peter was threatening to sell the babies to his friends, so Mary was looking forward to some frantic phone calls from the school mums later that day.

It wasn't until she'd dropped off the kids and boiled the kettle that she was able to turn her mind back to the matter of murder. Walker hadn't let her know of any developments in the case, which could just mean he wasn't allowed to tell her anything, but they hadn't arrested anyone as Mary had been keeping an eye on the news. Bernie would probably say it was police incompetence that no real suspects had emerged for Tiana's death, but Mary wasn't so sure. She had been on the scene herself – discovered poor Tiana's body, even – and she had no idea who might have wanted to hurt her. Maybe it had been an accident, somehow.

But she didn't believe that. There were too many coincidences. The threatening letters, for one thing, and the murmurings of disquiet between the cast and crew of the show. It was sad to think that her favourite TV show had been the end result of so much backbiting and bickering.

She was just scrolling through the most recent posts on the *Vampyra* forum when her phone started to ring.

"We're going back to Glasgow this morning and you're driving," Bernie barked down the phone. "Finn's works' van is out of action so he's had to borrow my car."

"Fine. That means I choose the tunes though," Mary told her, although she knew it wouldn't happen. Bernie huffing through Mary's excellent music collection was kind of off-putting.

As it turned out, there was a special report on the radio about the death of Tiana, so they listened to that on their way to Glasgow. Mary reckoned that DI Macleod and the rest of them wouldn't be too pleased with the journalist's assessment of the case. There were two instances of the phrase 'lack of suspects' and even one 'desperate for leads'.

"Serves him right," Bernie said when Mary mentioned that the Inspector might feel aggrieved by the woman on the news. "Should have brought us in right from the start. I'm sure if we'd been there earlier we'd have it solved already."

"I don't see how I could have been there earlier," Mary said, smarting from this assessment. "Trust me, even you wouldn't have found the killer. Tiana had been killed off-stage and out of sight, and there were several thousand people in the vicinity who could have done it. Face it, Bernie, there's not much the police could have done differently."

Bernie didn't reply to this, but instead stared out of the window until they returned to the convention centre. Once they had parked in the horrifically expensive multistory, Mary was surprised to see that Bernie was taking them in the opposite direction from the centre.

"We're heading to the hotel," Bernie explained as Mary trotted after her. "One of my sister's pals works there and I asked her about all her famous guests. She said that Stefan Alderick is meant to be checking out today."

"Really? I'm surprised the police are allowing that."

Bernie shrugged. "I don't think they can officially keep every member of the cast here. Not without some sort of evidence.

But you know what these rich guys are like, if we let them get on the plane then we'll never see them again."

"You're not planning to kidnap him are you," Mary said, glancing at her friend's face.

"Don't be ridiculous. I'm just going to ask him about something Anetta said. She said there was a rumour that Tiana was one of his 'girls'. I just want to know if that's true, and if they had a closer relationship than he disclosed to the police."

Mary followed Bernie to the hotel reception, where her friend began a long negotiation to try and get the man behind the desk to give her Alderick's room number. While this was happening, Mary thought about what she knew of the man. *Vampyra* had been his biggest show to date. He's appeared on a couple of American soap operas and lasted a rather pitiful two weeks on the truly terrible Break-dancing with the Stars. He was always pictured with lots of pretty women, but no long-term girlfriend.

Whatever Bernie said to the man must have worked as she came back with her usual smug smile. "He won't give me the room number, but he did say that Alderick has a cab booked for ten minutes to take him to the airport. So if we wait here we should be able to catch him before he goes."

"I'm surprised he told you that."

"Oh, we're old friends. After we met yesterday I did some digging on our Receptionist, Thomas Macinally. According to my sister's pal, he's known for spending a wee bit too much time with one of the pastry chefs. Something he would rather his wife didn't find out about. Anyway, Thomas and I are now best of friends."

"Having his cake and eating it, right?" Mary chuckled.

"What?"

"Because he's shagging a pastry chef. Get it?"

"Oh I got it. I was just hoping I didn't."

Mary snapped her jaw shut. Sometimes Bernie was a total killjoy.

A man in a long, dramatic coat walked in through the automatic doors and headed for the restaurant. Something about his stride seemed familiar.

"Hang on a minute, that's Lord Gigorath!" Mary jiggled from one foot to the other in excitement. "God, I wish I hadn't left my hoodie at home. If only I could have got him to sign it."

"Gigorath? Where have I heard that stupid name before?" Bernie was frowning. "Hang on, that's the guy that Anetta said Tiana had got sacked."

"What?"

"Yeah, the rumour going around the set was that Tiana had arranged for his dismissal. Anetta reckoned that he wouldn't be too happy about it."

"I hadn't heard that," Mary replied. "Although it would make sense. Everyone in the fandom knows that Fletcher Moon was pissed off about getting killed off. Do we know why Tiana got him sacked?"

"Anetta didn't seem too sure, but did mention he had a reputation for being 'handsy'."

"Ugh," Mary pulled a face.

"Yeah. Another one. And they never seem to realise that it's not the seventies anymore and that sort of behaviour just won't fly."

"But killing Tiana like that… Do you think it's possible?"

"I think we have to consider it," Bernie said, staring at the man who had pulled out his phone and was scrolling through something. "Look, we need to at least talk to the guy. Reckon you can play the fangirl one more time? I'll stay here and stake out Alderick."

Mary grinned. For once, this was right in her wheelhouse. "No problem."

Leaving Bernie behind she strolled across the hotel foyer.

"Excuse me, it's Mr Moon, isn't it?"

Lord Gigorath swept around and gave her a smile. Only close up it wasn't Gigorath, of course. It was just a man on the wrong side of sixty who chose to look at Mary's chest before her face. Nice.

"May I guess, you would like an autograph?"

Unlike his character on screen, Fletcher Moon had the sort of posh English accent that spoke of cream teas and boarding schools. If he hadn't been such an obvious creep, Mary might have felt intimidated. As it was, she thought of poor Tiana's broken body and fixed on a smile.

"Actually, I would love to buy you a coffee. Or something stronger if it's not too early."

The man made a show of checking his watch.

"Nearly eleven. The day that eleven o'clock is too early for a brandy is the day they can bury me in the ground."

"Haha," Mary laughed dutifully.

They walked together towards the restaurant where Moon looked disappointed when she matched his whiskey with nothing stronger than an English breakfast tea. Still, it didn't stop him from waxing lyrical about his life in acting, starting chronologically with his first appearance for the Royal Shakespeare Company in the nineteen-eighties.

"I played Hamlet in 1980, my debut. I think I've been chasing that high ever since. Did I tell you about my first visit to the Big Apple? That was in the nineties and…"

Reading between the lines, Mary got the picture of a man who had never quite lived up to the dream he had imagined for himself. Never an award winner, never recognised by the critics, she wondered how the man felt that his most recognisable role was on such a low-rent show. But how to ask him without insulting the man?

It turned out that she needn't have worried. When she asked about *Vampyra*: 'quite a career departure for you,' the man's ego was so large that he didn't view it as an insult. On the contrary, he seemed to almost regard his role as a charitable act.

"It lent the show credibility, you see dear," Moon explained. "To have a name like mine attached. The producers practically begged me to take the role. And I like to think I managed to elevate what was, frankly, some altogether average writing."

"It must have felt like a betrayal then, when they wrote you out of the show," Mary said.

A flicker of irritation passed over his face. "Oh, I wouldn't say that."

"Really?" Mary leaned forward. "You weren't disappointed, then? I mean, when they decided to kill your character off."

"These things happen in show business all the time, my dear. If I was upset every time I missed out on an audition, or had my lines cut, then that would be a very sad way to live."

"A lot of the fans thought it was terrible the way they treated you," Mary said, not willing to be fobbed off by his comments. "There were rumours that someone in the cast had it in for you."

"Was there indeed." Some of the levity had left the actor's manner. "Tell me dear, what is it that you do again?"

"Oh, nothing much. I'm a stay at home mum, and I just took some time away from the kids to attend the conference."

"A true fan."

"Exactly. I was at the panel where the… where all the awfulness happened."

Moon finished his drink. "It was a terrible accident."

"An accident? Tiana Schmidt was killed."

"Ah yes, but the incident on stage had nothing to do with that. No doubt some foolish technician forgot to use his screwdriver the right way around."

The actor stood up and started to pull on his coat. Mary had found the entire conversation odd. Why was he so sure that the lighting rig accident had nothing to do with Tiana's death? She was sure that the police hadn't made that information public.

"Thank you for the drink, my dear. Here's my card. I do hope you'll stay in touch," he said finally, with a face that said otherwise.

Mary left the restaurant and found Bernie standing outside.

"How did you get on?" she asked.

"Not sure yet. He seemed a bit shifty when asked about the show, but that could just be because they sacked him. There was one funny thing. Moon seemed sure that the lighting rig failure had nothing to do with Tiana's death."

"Why would he think that?"

"I'm not sure yet," Mary said. She wanted to think it over before she rushed to any conclusions. "Did you manage to speak to Alderick?"

"Only for about five seconds before he jumped into a taxi. He said that he had never been with Tiana, it was all just rumours. In fact, the whole thing about him being a womaniser was cooked up when he worked on a soap opera. Apparently his management company liked the publicity, but he's never been interested in that sort of thing."

"Huh. And do we just take our word for it?"

"We might as well," Bernie said. "I got a bit shirty with him, telling him that the police would cancel his passport if he was a suspect."

"Can they do that?"

"How the hell would I know? Anyway, at that point he told me that the reason he wasn't into womanising was that he'd been living with his partner, Evan, for three years and that he had absolutely no interest in Tiana or any other woman for that matter."

"Ah."

"We could follow it up, of course, but he knows it's an easy thing to check." Bernie led them out of the hotel. "Where next?"

"Let's get some lunch," Mary said. "I'm starving."

"All right. But after that we go and speak to the coppers. We can tell them about our interviews today and see if they've found anything out themselves. Not that I've got much faith in that."

"You never do, Bernie."

"Damn right."

Chapter 25: Bernie

People often accused Bernie Paterson of being weird about food. And it was true, since her 'incredible weight-loss journey' as it was termed in the local paper, she had certain firm views on carbs and refined sugar. But part of the problem was that she found food itself interminably dull. Time spent cooking was time she could use for other things. What Bernie Paterson most wished for in life was a sci-fi style food pill that you could take once a day and not have to worry about eating at all.

For Mary, it was the opposite. The woman seemed to spend her whole day thinking about food, what to eat and when. After their interviews at the conference hotel, they had ended up in an up-market bistro in the West End of Glasgow for lunch where Mary ordered some dreadful Asian fusion dish that was all fried chicken and sugary sauces. How the woman wasn't the size of a house, Bernie would never know.

At least they made a decent salad, she thought, and they had managed to do her some grilled chicken to go with it. But the hour and a half spent on eating, chatting and eating some more could have been spent much more productively. As it was, they didn't make it to the police station at Govan to meet with Macleod until nearly two o'clock.

"This is a bit bigger than Invergryff, isn't it," Mary said as they walked into the lobby.

"Still smells like microwaved tea and desperation," Bernie replied as they went to speak to the constable on the front desk. The whole room had been sadly infiltrated by 'modern policing', including posters about how to snitch on your neighbours and information about something called 'community policing', which made Bernie's teeth itch. Police officers were, to Bernie, a necessary evil, and trying to pretend that they were cuddly teddy bears was the worst kind of political stupidity.

Macleod came to collect them and brought them upstairs. If Bernie had been of a suspicious nature – and of course she was – then she might have thought that the Detective Inspector wanted to keep them away from the main office. She could have called him out on it, but for once she decided not to push her luck. They were only allowing her and Mary to observe the upcoming interview because they had delivered the suspect wrapped in a bow.

Sadly, this was one of the modern interview suites where they watched the interviews in a room of TV screens rather than the good old-fashioned two-way mirror. Bernie preferred the earlier type where you felt like you could stare into the suspect's eyes. As it was, they just had to watch on a screen at an unsettling jaunty angle when Macleod brought Fletcher Moon into the room.

"Has it started yet?" Walker asked as he arrived. Now that Mary's worse half had arrived there were four of them in the cramped observation station. Only the young uniformed constable in front of the screens was allowed to control the feed, and he had got quite shirty when Bernie had tried to do some zooming in.

"What did Moon say when you arrested him?" Bernie asked.

"He's not under arrest yet, we just asked him to come in for questioning. But I would say he seemed nervous, a little too polite, that sort of thing."

"I bet he didn't stare at your boobs," Mary said darkly.

"Not that I noticed," Walker replied.

Bernie hushed them as Macleod started to do the introductions for the tape. In a surprising moment, Fletcher Moon introduced himself under two names, the one they knew and his birth name of Frederick David Mullins, born in Oldham.

"I had to posh up for the RSC, you see," the man explained. If he thought that the coppers would be impressed by the name-dropping of his acting credentials, then he was wrong.

It didn't take Macleod long to get to the point. "Mr Moon, we were made aware that there were some allegations that the late Tiana Schmidt was responsible for your resignation from the television show. Is that correct?"

"There are always rumours around the set. Hollywood thrives on it. No, the producers and I reached a mutual understanding. To be honest, I had rather outgrown the show. Or, to be exact, it was always somewhat beneath me. But sometimes one has to take a part for the money, especially when one is no longer twenty-five."

Mary stifled a giggle, and Bernie couldn't help but agree that the man was making himself ridiculous. He hadn't seen twenty-five in this millennium.

"It's interesting that you should say that," Macleod said. "We spoke to the Executive Producer just an hour ago. He confirmed that Tiana Schmidt had made an informal complaint about your behaviour. Apparently she had objected to being called 'love' on set."

"Rather snowflake behaviour, don't you think?"

"You could argue that, Mr Moon. However, it was your reaction to being called out on this that Tiana most objected to. Mr Ashley told us that when you heard she had objected to your language you said it was just what you would expect from a –

Here the DI read out two words that were so offensive they drew audible gasps from Bernie and Mary. Macleod continued the questioning, unfazed.

"Miss Schmidt had a Jewish father and a Hispanic mother, as we understand it, so you made sure to insult both racial heritages, didn't you?"

You couldn't tell on the grainy screens, but Bernie reckoned the man had just turned pale.

"I… I was under considerable stress at the time. I have a record from my Doctor to evidence my poor mental health."

Bernie clicked her tongue at that one.

"It doesn't seem to me that that excuses offensive language,

Mr Moon."

"No. I made a dreadful mistake. I told Miss Schmidt that I was sorry if I had offended her. I apologised in person, but she was quite... unreasonable about it."

"In what way?"

Moon folded his arms across his chest. "She wanted a public apology in front of the entire crew. Well, it would have been an admission of guilt. Can you imagine what the internet would have done if I'd been branded a racist? It would have ended my career."

There was a distinct lack of sympathy in the room.

"Anyway, I came to an arrangement with the blasted woman. I would leave the show at the end of the season and nothing more would be said about it. Ha! I know fine well she didn't stick to her end of the bargain. I've not been offered a single role since. That woman has poisoned the whole industry against me."

"You must have been very angry with Miss Schmidt."

"I was bloody furious. But if you think I'm the kind of person who goes around murdering people, you've got another thing coming."

"It does seem like of all the people at the convention you had the best motive for her death."

"That doesn't matter a jot when there's not a whisper of evidence that I touched that woman."

Macleod nodded to DS Sangar who passed over a file of papers.

"It's interesting that you mention evidence, Mr Moon, because my team has been working on just that very thing. You'll note that we took fingerprints from you today. In examining the defective lighting rig in the convention centre we discovered a single fingerprint on one of the damaged hinges. That print came up as a match for your right index finger."

Now the actor looked like he was going to be sick. "I don't… I don't know how that got there."

"Right. And I don't suppose you've heard of anyone with the internet username spv1980 or 1980newjob? Interesting the use of the year 1980 isn't it? One might assume it to be someone's date of birth. Or perhaps the year that something important happened. Like the first time they played Hamlet."

Moon groaned. "You lot have bloody spies everywhere, don't you."

"I would like to tell you a little story," Macleod said. "And as you're not yet under caution, you can understand that a lot of this is supposition. But I'm picturing a very angry man spouting off online about a TV show that fired him. And then he discovers that the members of the crew, including the one that got him fired in the first place are coming to Glasgow. So he starts sending nasty wee letters to them, only that isn't enough for him. He decides to sabotage the stage that they are to speak on. Only while he is damaging the lighting rig, the young woman surprises him. Maybe he didn't intend to kill her. But it happens anyway. You're an actor, Mr Moon. Is this a convincing script?"

"No! I mean, not the last part. Oh god, what was I thinking." He buried his head in his hands. Macleod and Sangar exchanged a look.

"I think it's time we cautioned you and you got in contact with a lawyer, Mr Moon," the Detective Inspector said.

"Wait," the actor said, his voice trembling. "I'll cop to the sabotage. And the letters. I just wanted to call out the other people on the show. Not one of them stuck up for me, none would answer my calls after I left. Especially that bitch Anetta. I got that woman her first role you know."

"What happened on Sunday," Macleod prompted.

"I damaged the rig. When you've spent five decades on set like I have, then you get to learn how these things work. I knew it would break at some point during the panel. But I didn't want to hurt anyone. I thought it would get us some publicity, maybe put me back in the good graces of some producers for a while. I didn't even know that Tiana was there until the news came out that someone had killed her. I swear!"

He dissolved into loud, wet sobs and Macleod ended the interview. A stunned silence had fallen on the people in the observation room.

"He's still a suspect," Walker said eventually, but Bernie knew that his heart wasn't in it.

"Aye, you can tell the media that he's still under arrest," she told him. "And it might buy you some time, make you look like the investigation is going well. But we both know that cretin didn't kill anyone. He's not the type to get his hands dirty."

Walker sighed. "Possibly not. I don't suppose you want to tell me who did do it?"

Bernie wasn't sure if he was joking or not. "I haven't worked that out yet."

"You surprise me."

"But I'm sure I will. And I'll do it before any of your lot."

"That's great," Walker rubbed at his eyes. "Because I'm knackered. And unlike the WWC I have to make sure that everything is done to the letter of the law. Which means I have a lot of paperwork to do concerning Mr Moon's confession. You wouldn't like to leave me to it, would you?"

"Fine. I'll call you when I've got the killer."

"You do that," Walker replied, but Bernie could tell his heart wasn't in it. Poor lad. He seemed a little fed up. She couldn't imagine why.

Chapter 26: Liz

"Got him! Yes!" Liz had never felt the need to punch the air before, not being a natural athlete, but right at this moment she felt like she'd won a penalty shoot-out, a hundred-metre final and the last point at Wimbledon, all rolled into one.

"Everything all right dear," Dave called through from the kitchen.

"I've only bloody well found Ryan Porter's dad," Liz told him, heading through to give her husband a cuddle.

"That's nice," Dave replied. "Who was that again?"

It must be nice to be so oblivious, Liz thought, even if it was infuriating for her as a partner. "The Porter/Michelson case, remember. Ryan won't marry Kaylie until he discovers who his biological father is."

"Sounds like something out of Eastenders," Dave said.

"It does a bit. Anyway, none of that matters because I've only gone and found him."

Seeing as Dave wasn't getting her enthusiasm, Liz picked up her phone and called Bernie instead.

"We've just come out of Govan police station," Bernie said before Liz could speak. "They're going to charge Fletcher Moon with attempted murder, although I reckon the judge will bring it down to a lesser sentence. The stupid sod was just cross about losing his job and decided to take it out on the rest of them."

"But he didn't do the murder?"

"Nah. A racist and a coward but not a murderer. At least that's what I told the DI at the station."

"Huh." Yet again, Liz was getting all the less exciting jobs. When was the last time she'd been inside a police station? It was all well and good being the one that was best at research and accounting but it meant that you always ended up doing – well – all the research and accounting.

"What were you calling about?"

"Oh yeah." Liz's news didn't sound quite so exciting anymore. "I discovered who Ryan Porter's father is and I know where he is now."

"That's brilliant," Bernie replied. "Who the hell is he?"

Pleased by her friend's clear enthusiasm at the result, Liz explained to her where her research had led. "I worked out that in Polish Marty can be short for Martyn, just like in English we have the same name but with an 'in'. And that made me wonder if he had ever anglicised his name. A search for Martin Gortat brought up one result, from the census of 2011. At the time he was living just outside Nottingham."

"And you think this is our guy?"

"Yeah. The age is right. The bad news for Ryan is that he was living with a woman of the same surname and three children."

Liz could sense Bernie thinking this over on the other end of the phone.

"Let's wait and tell him until we're certain."

"Right. And I'm not sure what we should say about the siblings. I mean, they're Ryan's half brothers and sisters, aren't they? Are we really the right people to break that sort of news to him?"

"I'll leave the ethical stuff to you," Bernie said firmly. "Look, we're just about finished here. For some reason Macleod won't let us watch any more interviews. Honestly, the guy acts like he's doing us a favour when their case would be dead in the ground without the WWC."

"You didn't say that to him, did you?"

"Might have mentioned it. Anyway, Mary is sticking around to make moon eyes at her boyfriend, so I'm heading home."

Liz checked her notes. "I was thinking I might speak to Kaylie today. Sound her out about the car crash."

"Do you think that's wise? She is a paying client after all. One of only two at the moment, might I remind you. And she might not like you bringing up her dead boyfriend."

"I know. But what if Linda is right about the crash? What if it wasn't a simple accident? Maybe there's something Kaylie could tell us about that night. She was meant to be Lenny's girlfriend after all."

"You're not doing this because you're sulking about Mary and

I getting a murder case are you?"

Liz resisted the urge to throw the phone across the room, but only just. "Bernie, when have I ever wasted your time? If I didn't think there was something off about this car crash then I wouldn't be looking into it."

"That's good enough for me," her friend replied. "Let's meet at Kaylie's place in an hour. We can go to update her on the wedding postponement, and if the conversation happens to turn to the death of her former boyfriend, then so be it."

Liz ended the call and realised she was still in her pyjamas. Working for the WWC was definitely getting her into bad habits. When she had worked at a high level in an insolvency firm she was never seen without a suit and a pair of heels. Mind you, it was nice to roll out of bed five minutes before she started work. And PJs were much more forgiving if the toddler threw up on them.

Still, if she was going to be asking a bereaved woman about her dead boyfriend, Liz wanted to at least look professional. She spent most of the hour before meeting Bernie getting ready, putting on a smart dress with a paisley print and doing her hair. She had recently had a protective style done so she just swept the braids up into a high bun. She nodded at herself in the mirror. Perfectly presentable and no toddler sick. Excellent.

Kaylie's place was a flat in a modern complex in the centre of town. It was one of the streets that had been pretty rough a few years back and had now been 'gentrified', with only a few vape shops and some confused-looking men in trench-coats and slippers wandering about to suggest that it wasn't quite as posh as it seemed.

Bernie was already outside, doing some weird lunge-type exercises next to her car.

"What on earth are you doing?"

"I missed a gym session today. Every minute sat on your arse is a minute less on your life expectancy."

"You just made that one up," Liz told her.

"I'm sure I read it somewhere. Anyway, well done on tracking down Marty Gortat."

"Thanks. I've done some more digging on him. As far as I can tell he's still in the Nottingham area. One of his daughters, Fiona Gortat, has some social media pages and they show a few pictures of her dad. I was waiting until I spoke to you to find out what to do next."

Bernie shrugged. "We'll have to tell Ryan. And I can't see how we do it without mentioning his dad's new family. After all, he's only going to do an internet search himself."

"True."

"At least Kaylie should get some good news. No need to postpone the wedding now."

Liz wasn't so sure. She had never been convinced that Ryan's only reason for stopping the wedding was the dad thing.

"I guess we'll find out. Ready to go upstairs?"

"Yep. Oh before we go in, there's something else I need to tell you," Bernie said. "A funny thing happened this morning. And by funny, I mean not at all amusing. Kaylie Michelson's debit card was declined so she couldn't pay our bill."

"Is that right?"

"Yeah, she had to phone Daddy to get an advance. But you know there's nothing I like less than a client without the ability to pay."

Liz thought back to her research on the family. "She does like fancy things. Her car's pretty flashy for a start."

"Dad pays for that," Bernie shook her head. "Ryan Porter's mother told me so. She's not the biggest fan of her potential daughter-in-law."

Something was nagging at Liz. "I mean, she's a gym receptionist, so she's not exactly well paid, but I wonder why Daddy keeps having to bail her out so much. Where's her money going?"

"Maybe she just spends it on rubbish. You know, takeaways, fancy clothes, it all adds up."

They had reached Kaylie's flat and pressed on the buzzer until they were allowed in. The flat itself was on the third floor and Kaylie showed them into a small but artfully decorated living room. Liz found herself staring at the furniture and the woman's clothes, trying to work out where her money was going. Everything seemed quite new, but not designer names or anything. Apart from her handbag, which Liz knew that

Ryan had bought for her as she'd seen the gushing post on social media.

"I've just come off the phone with the caterer," Kaylie told them as they sat down. "I'm hoping you've come with good news because those langoustines aren't going to wait."

Liz blinked to dislodge that rather peculiar image.

"We do have some good news. We've been working with Ryan on his personal reasons for postponing the wedding."

"Which you still won't tell me," Kaylie pouted.

"I wouldn't be fair to your fiancé to do so," Bernie explained. Liz was impressed with her friend's patience. It was amazing how Bernie could tone down her, well, Bernieness for a paying client. "But my colleague and I are going to speak to him later and we're hopeful that the wedding will be back on soon."

"About bloody time. Honestly, the whole thing has just been so draining. I had to take this week off work with stress."

Bernie's smile became more fixed. "They are lucky to have such an honest employee," she said.

"We did want to ask you something," Liz said, deciding it was time to bite the bullet. "When we were doing our background research something came up. We didn't realise that your boyfriend before Ryan, Lenny Ingot, had passed away."

Kaylie's face shut down. It was weird, like something had just switched off inside her.

"That was a really bad time for me," she said, spitting out each word like it was a monumental effort. "I had to, like, have a whole lot of therapy afterwards. I don't like talking about it."

"Sure," Liz said, and she did feel genuinely bad for bringing it up. Kaylie was upset, and maybe the fact that she hadn't plastered her grief all over social media meant that she had felt her sadness on the inside. And who could blame her for wanting to move on quickly with Ryan.

As if Kaylie knew what Liz was thinking, the young woman rubbed at her eyes. "God, it was a total nightmare. I think that's why I was so happy when Ryan proposed. It was a way to move on, leave all the Lenny drama behind me."

Looking around the room, Liz noticed that there weren't many photos of Ryan, just one of them on holiday where Kaylie was posing in a skimpy swimsuit. In contrast, there were two photographs of her standing in front of a huge black car.

"That was my baby, my Range Rover," Kaylie said when she noticed Liz looking at the pictures. "But it was getting too expensive to keep so I had to sell it."

"Your dad bought you the new car, didn't he? Good of him to help out," Bernie said.

"Aye, well, I'll always be his little girl, won't I? And besides, the new car is much more economical. And it's still cute enough to be insta-worthy."

Liz could see Bernie twitching at the phrase. Poor Kaylie, she didn't really make it easy to like her. What exactly was it that attracted Ryan Porter to this woman? Mind you, Liz thought, if we knew why people went for awful partners, life would definitely be a lot easier.

"We better get going," Bernie said.

"Yeah, like I said, I've got to speak to the caterer. She's trying to tell me I don't need a sweet trolley, but all the weddings in the magazines have them."

"A sweet trolley?" Bernie's bottom eyelid had started to flicker. "This is on top of all the cake and desserts and everything."

Liz clutched her friend's arm. Time to leave before the bomb went off.

"Thanks for your time," she told Kaylie as she headed for the door.

"An entire trolley of sweets," Bernie hissed as they closed the flat door behind them. "Just what people need after all that overindulgence. What is the world coming to?"

"I know," Liz said soothingly. "Let's just get you back to the car."

Bernie was still jabbering on about society's addiction to sugar when she started the engine.

"Here's something that might cheer you up. I grabbed this on the way out," Liz said, holding up an envelope. "Let's see what her latest bank statement says."

"How very unethical of you," Bernie crowed. "I'm so proud."

Liz ignored this. In truth, she didn't feel too good about it, but her curiosity had got the better of her. She ripped the envelope open.

"Just like we thought. Well into her overdraught and it looks like she's got at least one maxed-out credit card. I'll take a closer look at it when I get home and see if I can work out what she's spending her money on."

Liz glanced up as they pulled out of the parking space to see Kaylie watching them from the window. She had her phone to her ear and was clearly shouting at someone. Was she just what she appeared? A bit of an airhead who liked her life to look like the influencers she saw online. Or was there something else going on? Liz didn't really believe in gut feelings, but something in her stomach was telling her that Kaylie was hiding something.

Chapter 27: Walker

It was almost pleasing how closely Tony Ashley fitted the image of a big Hollywood producer. If only he had been smoking a cigar, then Walker would have felt the man had truly embodied the stereotype.

"It's not that I only care about the money," the man was telling them, a glass of whiskey in one hand punctuating each sentence, "it's that if I don't care about the money, then nothing ever gets made. That's what everyone in this industry forgets."

Macleod was sitting with his eyes half-shut and Walker wasn't sure if it was boredom or contempt for the man in the room. They were sitting in Ashley's hotel room as he had 'respectfully declined' to go down to the station, and without any evidence against the man they couldn't arrest him. Now that they had ruled out Fletcher Moon, they were back to having no credible suspects. Ashley had risen to the top of the list purely for being Tiana's boss.

"You should have told us that you had seen Tiana not long before she died," Macleod told the man, ignoring the industry small talk.

"Ah, yes, I probably should have said something. But you see I didn't realise she had died so soon after I spoke to her. I had the impression that she had been killed in the unfortunate accident on the stage. How did the poor woman die?"

"We are not at liberty to reveal that, I'm afraid," Walker said, taking over the mantel from Macleod. "Do you think you could tell us exactly what happened when you met with Tiana that day?"

"It was hardly a meeting. I bumped into her not long before the panel and she had taken it on herself to get a little break. Well, I knew that Anetta was waiting for her make-up, so I told Tiana to make her way over there."

"We have a witness that stated you were angry with her. That you raised your voice and behaved in a forceful manner."

Ashley shrugged. "It was a busy day and Tiana was running late. So yeah, maybe I came across as a bit agitated. But I'm passionate about my work and I can't stand when people aren't as committed as I am."

"You think Tiana wasn't committed? We had heard she was well-known for her work." Walker knew that Mary at least had regarded her as one of the best MUAs in the business.

"Oh, she was fine on set, I suppose. A bit prone to throwing her weight around."

"Like with Fletcher Moon?"

Ashley shifted in his seat. "I already told you, Moon was a well known creep. I mean, you just can't get away with that stuff anymore."

Was he imagining it, or did the producer look wistful? "But you did sack Moon because of Tiana's allegations, right?"

"Yeah. If the man had kept his stupid mouth shut he'd have got away with a slap on the wrist. But Tiana wouldn't let anything like that slide. Not that she should have to, of course," Ashley added after a slightly too long pause.

"So you weren't annoyed with Tiana for causing trouble on set?"

"Not at all. To be honest, Fletcher Moon was a liability. Too expensive, too prone to telling the Director his job. I was glad to have a reason to get rid of the man."

Macleod steered the conversation back to the Sunday. "On the day of Miss Schmidt's death, you met her at the coffee cart and that's where you had your argument, right?"

"Like I told you it wasn't an argument. But yes, I walked her from the coffee stand to the area next to the panel."

"You never went into the backstage area with her?"

"No. They had a separate room for the panel members where we could get a bottle of water and some horrible pre-packaged snacks. It's true that you Brits have dreadful food."

The police officers ignored this insult.

"And when you left Tiana, she seemed fine?"

"Of course. A little irritated that I had told her to get the hell on with her work. But like I said, it wasn't a falling out or anything. I just didn't want Anetta getting on my case if they were running late. And if I'm honest, I was a bit pissed off that she was drinking on the job."

"Drinking?" Walker looked at Macleod who returned his blank stare. "No one else suggested that Tiana had been drinking."

"Well they can't have got close enough to her. She was slurring her words and everything. I told her to God damn pull herself together or she'd be out of a job. I could get a dozen kids fresh out of beauty school for the wages I was paying her."

Macleod leaned forward, his large hands on the table. "I want you to tell us exactly why you thought that Miss Schmidt was intoxicated."

Belatedly, the producer seemed unsure of himself. "Oh, well, it's not exactly uncommon in this industry. And these conventions are boring as hell. Like I said, she just seemed off, slurring her words and I think she had to put a hand on the wall, like she was steadying herself."

"Did you smell any alcohol on her?"

He frowned. "Now that you mention it, I didn't. But then, there are ways to cover that up aren't there, the odd breath mint before work, we've all done that haven't we?"

This was met with stony silence.

"Well, maybe I was wrong about the drinking. My point is that I had no reason to kill the poor girl. If anything, her death causes me a recruitment problem for next season."

"You just said she was easily replaced," Walker reminded him.

"In a normal production, sure. But *Vampyra* is getting a

reputation. You know what the internet is like. They're calling it a 'cursed set'. Someone even mentioned *The Crow* the other day for God's sake. Tiana's death is a serious headache for all of us."

"It was certainly a headache for her," Macleod said softly.

Tony Asher looked horrified. "That wasn't what I meant."

"Of course not. Besides, one death is hardly a curse. I would imagine it won't hurt your advertising at all."

"Ah, well there was the unfortunate incident at the end of season two."

The two police officers waited for him to elaborate.

Ashley coughed. "A young intern died. Nothing to do with the show, I have to say. He was found at home, a heroin overdose. Very sad."

Macleod's face was serious. "His name?"

"Charles Midhurst. Went by Chuck, if I'm remembering right. Like I said, he was just a kid. He'd only worked on the show for a couple of weeks. I barely even knew him. In fact, I don't think I knew his name until he died. The production company paid for the funeral."

"But not because you were guilty of anything?" Walker suggested.

Ashley gulped down his drink. "I don't like that insinuation. In fact, if we were in the States I would sue you for slander."

"Just stick to the facts, please, Mr Ashley."

"That's as much as I know. The kid didn't even hang out with anyone on the show. He was a runner for us during the day, partying with his friends at night. It was his stupid friends that got him into trouble. And then I guess he couldn't get himself out of it."

Ashley looked a little green in the face, and Walker could tell he was already regretting having brought up the boys death. Although on the face of it, there didn't seem to be much of a connection with Tiana Schmidt.

"Did they know each other, Tiana and Midhurst?" Macleod asked, his words echoing Walker's thoughts.

"Don't see why they would have," Ashley replied.

"Well, if anything occurs to you, please get in touch. And maybe don't book that flight back to the US just yet."

"Fine," Ashley glared at them. "But if I get food poisoning from another tasteless portion of fish and chips, I'm going to sue every last one of you."

Chapter 28: Mary

Mary had been looking forward to spending some quality time with Walker, but when she managed to meet up with him at the convention centre on Tuesday afternoon, he looked dead on his feet.

"Sorry if I'm bad company," he said putting two takeaway cups on the table for them. They were back in the café space where Mary had met with Tiana on the day she died. It was hard not to be freaked out by that fact, but Mary was doing her best to pretend that she was fine. Besides, Walker looked like he was the one who needed comforting at the moment.

"It must be a difficult case for the police," Mary said.

"That's the understatement of the year. Do you know that Macleod got tripped up by one of those awful photographers on his way in this morning? When he fell over I thought he was having another collapse."

Mary reached out and laced her fingers with his. She knew how upset Walker had been when Macleod had ended up in hospital from his first diabetic hypo.

"It's hard to get rid of that fear, isn't it? Even if he's managing fine now."

"Oh, he seems hale and hearty. He certainly was when he gave that paparazzi a piece of his mind, I can tell you that. I reckon if I hadn't pulled him away he would have socked the cameraman one on the chin."

Mary's lips quirked into a smile at the thought. "It must make your job harder, having to deal with the press."

"It's more difficult for Macleod and DCI Allen. Because we're only sergeants, we just have to make sure we don't go shooting our mouths off to anyone. Leaks are deadly in these sorts of cases, not to mention career ending."

She shifted in her seat. "You know that you can trust Bernie and me, don't you?"

A flush crept up his neck in that schoolboy way that always made her heart lift.

"Oh, I didn't mean you two. I mean, Bernie drives me crazy, but I know that she's trustworthy."

"That's because she doesn't believe in lying," Mary explained. "That's why it's important never to ask her questions like 'what do you think of my new haircut' or 'is my singing voice okay'."

A group of students took a table near them and started chatting loudly. The conference centre was due to host a University open day that afternoon. After having so much of the building given over to the investigation, it was strange to see things going back to normal.

"We're relocating to Govan police station," Walker said, his mind clearly on the same thing. "They're closing the incident room here. The DCI keeps saying it doesn't mean they're allocating less resources to the case, but it still feels like a bit of a failure."

"You got Fletcher Moon," Mary said, trying to make him feel better. "That should count for something."

Walker just grunted at that idea.

"I feel like we're getting somewhere on the case," Mary continued. "Even if it might not look like it. We are starting to understand the dynamics of the *Vampyra* cast and crew. And that's got to count for something."

"Unless Tiana's killer has nothing to do with the show," Walker suggested. "Just some random psychopath."

"You don't believe that, do you?"

He shook his head. "No. If someone wanted to cause fear, he would have gone for one of the stars. The choice of a make-up artist is too unusual. I think she was killed by someone she knew, for some reason that we haven't discovered yet."

"I do too." Mary took a sip of her tea. It was dreadful, even though she had added four sachets of sugar.

"Even the timeline isn't too great," Walker said. "The CCTV turned out to be a total bust. Twelve camera feeds and none of them anywhere near the murder site. So I've been checking all the definite timings and sightings of our victim since we interviewed Ashley. He saw Tiana less than an hour after you saw her and he thought she seemed inebriated. But you thought she was fine."

"She was," Mary was sure on this point at least. "She was talking quite clearly, no sign of any impairment."

"And none of the others on the panel spoke to her before they went on stage, so I can't get confirmation of what Ashley saw."

Mary tried to picture the scene, but it was still too confusing. "The others saw Tiana when they needed their make-up done, didn't they."

"No. Tiana never got to them, despite Ashley having a go at her."

Mary frowned. "You must have that wrong. Tiana must have done Anetta's make-up at least."

Walker shook his head. "No, Tiana never made it over to Anetta. Anetta told us that she waited a bit for the make-up artist, then when Tiana didn't show she had to do it herself."

"No, that can't be right," Mary started to puzzle it through. "Tiana did Anetta's make-up that day."

"Not according to the statements."

"Anetta was in her *Vampyra* dress. There's a certain type of scale tattoo that goes up her neck. You remember it from the TV show? And one of the things that Tiana is famous for is that she draws it fresh every time. Tiana did it for her before the panel. I saw it."

Walker leaned back in his chair and stared at her. "Maybe she did it earlier on?"

"Possible, I suppose, but the whole point of the special paint is that it glows most when it's fresh. I read an article about it."

"Of course you did." He kissed her and Mary knew that she had cheered him up. "You're a funny little nerdy thing, aren't you?"

"Yes. But listen, you need to go and speak to Anetta again. Because if she is saying that Tiana didn't do her make-up then she's lying."

"And it would be good to find out why," Walker nodded. "I'll send Macleod a message."

Mary poured the last dregs of the terrible tea down her throat. "It's not been quite the conference I was imagining. I thought I was going to be part of this silly fandom where we could all forget all our problems with dragons and vampires and all that stuff. But now it's like the whole show will always be tainted by what I've learned about the people involved. Apart from Tiana, I'm not sure there's much to like about any of them."

"You can still love the show," Walker said. "I mean, there's plenty of examples of writers and actors being horrible people, but still making great art."

"True," Mary agreed, but she knew in her heart she would probably never watch the show again. Rationally, it shouldn't matter but emotionally it did.

"I'm sorry you're involved in all this," Walker said.

"It is my job," Mary replied a little stiffly.

"I know. But it's just sad that it's ruined your special weekend. It's not like you get much time to yourself."

"Or time together. Is it weird that most of the time we spend together is because someone has been murdered?"

Walker gave her a lopsided grin. "I try not to think about that too much."

"Probably wise. How about a vintage Star Trek marathon when this is all over? I picked up a load of DVDs some dealer was trying to get rid of."

"Sounds perfect."

Chapter 29: Bernie

Bernie was pulling off a particularly difficult manoeuvre with a pair of dumbbells and her treadmill when she heard someone hammering on the door. Pulling off her headphones she grabbed one of the weights and went cautiously down the stairs.

Surely a delivery man would have given up by now, she thought as the door banged again. Then to her horror, it started to open. She held the dumbbell high so that she could take on any assailant and prepared to leap down the stairs.

"Aargh!"

"Bloody hell Liz!"

Liz held up her hands in surrender. "I used the spare key. Why didn't you answer the doorbell?"

"I was doing my weight bearing aerobics," Bernie said. "Finn says I have to wear headphones because the music annoys the neighbours. You're lucky I didn't smash your head in."

"Thanks, I feel really lucky."

"Go and grab yourself a cuppa," Bernie told her. "I'll get a quick shower."

"You better be quick. I've got something good to tell you."

Liz wouldn't say anything else until Bernie had got out of her lycras, so she showered in record time and pulled on some clean clothes. When she came down the stairs she saw that Liz had her laptop out and was fidgeting with excitement.

"Well, come on then, tell me all about it."

"I traced the ownership of Kaylie's Range Rover," Liz said, getting straight to the point. "Remember how she told us it was her baby but she'd had to sell it? I couldn't get it out of my head. Anyway, tracing it wasn't that hard. There's only one registered dealer in Invergryff and he's a pal of Dave's. A fellow golfer."

Liz and Bernie shared an eye-roll at men and their love of hitting balls with sticks.

"Anyway, the Range Rover guy told me that he had sold Kaylie the car in the first place. Cost her sixty grand, would you believe it. Reckon that daddy stumped up most of the money?"

"I wouldn't bet you a fiver against it."

"Yeah. But here's the thing. The guy from the garage was pissed off about it, because when she came to sell it on, she did it privately. Not through the garage."

"I guess that's not that unusual."

"No. But wait until you find out who she sold it to."

Fifteen minutes later they parked Liz's car outside a warehouse with a sign that read 'Allied Solutions Ltd'.

"Stupid name," Bernie commented.

"I thought so," Liz agreed.

Liz had told Bernie that Perrie Mellworth would be easy to crack, but that hadn't prepared her for the girl to burst into tears the moment they walked through the door.

"Come on, let's go outside," Liz told her. They walked out of the building and found a wooden bench nearby. Perrie brought out a disgusting smelling strawberry vape and started puffing away to calm down. Bernie resisted telling her about the health risks, but made a note to send the woman a link to some websites later.

"I knew you'd come back," Perrie said, her voice wobbling. "And I thought: maybe I could run away, go abroad or something. But I don't have a passport. And I'm scared of planes."

Bernie let Liz take the lead on this one. She knew that if she spoke to the woman in even her gentlest Bernie voice she would probably faint.

"I think that only works on the telly," Liz told her. "Besides, it would even make you look more guilty to the police."

"But I'm not guilty! At least, not in the way you think."

It was nice to have all your suspicions confirmed.

"We think we might know something about it. We've just been speaking to Kaylie Michelson."

That brought the waterworks back on. Bernie waited impatiently while Liz tapped the woman on the back and made comforting noises.

"Why don't you start with the party," Bernie said when her patience had run out. "And how you all left together."

"I wanted to go home early," Perrie said. "And I said I'd give them a lift."

"Lenny and Kaylie?"

"That's right. We lived in the same part of town so it made sense. Anyway, Kaylie started talking about how she wanted a shot of my car. She was demanding that I let her drive. I knew she had had a couple of drinks, but I had no idea that she was too drunk to control it."

"She wasn't just drunk, was she?"

Perrie flinched. "No. She was on coke. I mean, we all did a bit, but Kaylie was different. Always high, always pushing it on everyone else. And the day of the party she was totally off on one."

"And yet you let her drive you home."

"I know. But she was going on about it for ages. It just felt like we'd be fine. It wasn't far, just ten minutes on the motorway and we'd be home."

"But it didn't work out like that?"

"No. It was an accident though. That much was true. Lenny

and Kaylie had got into this argument about something stupid. The music on the radio, I don't know. I wasn't drinking as I had to get up early the next day for work, so they were doing my head in. I was just sort of leaning back against the back seat when the car started spinning. I honestly don't know if Lenny had tried to grab the wheel, or if Kaylie just lost it or what. But a second later we were in the barrier."

She took in a shaky breath. "I had never seen a dead body before, but as soon as we got out of the car, it was obvious that Lenny was dead. It's not like on the telly, is it? When people are dead they look really dead, you know."

"We know," Bernie replied. "Whose idea was it to say you were driving?"

"Oh, that was Kaylie. I mean, I was freaking out, saying we should phone an ambulance, even though there was nothing they could do. And then Kaylie sort of goes all quiet and cold, and she says, if they find out I was driving I'll go to jail. And it was like, she didn't have to ask, I just sort of said I would do it for her."

Bernie raised her eyebrows. "What, just out of the kindness of your own heart?"

"Well, I hadn't had a drink, you see, so we knew that I would pass the breathalyser but Kaylie reckoned she would fail. And poor Lenny was already dead, so what was the sense in ruining someone else's life."

"And the fact that she gave you her Range Rover had nothing to do with it?" Bernie snapped. "No, don't start the waterworks again, for God's sake."

The sniffling Perrie reluctantly admitted, that yes, she had taken Kaylie's car. It hadn't been a bribe or anything, more like a way of saying thank you. Bernie could tell by the way the woman glanced down at her feet that even Perrie didn't believe that one.

"What do I do now?" she said, raising her tear-filled eyes to them.

"Well, it's all going to come out. There's no point in lying anymore. But it might be worth going to the police before Kaylie does. Get your side of the story across first."

"I'll go now," Perrie said, wiping her nose on her sleeve.

"See that you do," Bernie said sternly. She watched the woman go and decided she would never call Mary a wet lettuce again. Even Mary Plunkett wouldn't do something so stupid just to be pals with someone and with the added bribe of a shiny new car. Perrie Mellworth would now go down in history as the wettest lettuce of all.

"Are we going to speak to Kaylie now?" Liz asked.

"You can bet your arse we are," Bernie replied. "And I'm going to enjoy this one. Even if it means we're losing a paying client."

"You're so selfless," Liz told her.

"Was that sarcasm?"

"Yes."

Back at Kaylie's flat, the woman let them in with a scowl. She had some sort of hair treatment in that meant her head was festooned with towels like a PG version of Medusa.

"You better be quick. I've to take this off in twenty minutes or I won't get me Keratin shine for the wedding."

Whatever sort of dreadful human being Kaylie-Ann Michelson might be, Bernie had to admit that her flat smelled delightful. She had some sort of posh room scent going on, although the fact that it seemed to puff steam randomly into the air was more than a little distracting. Like living with a tiny volcano.

"I was happy to see that your latest payment of our bills went through straightaway," Bernie said once they were all sat down together on the leather sofas. "But I did notice it came from a different account. Did your dad step in to help you again?"

"Yes," she shrugged. "He's always helped me out when I need it. I guess I was just a little short this month."

"Daddy's money has come in handy for lots of things, hasn't it?" Bernie prompted.

Kaylie narrowed her eyes. "Yeah, what's your point?"

"That Range Rover you had. Quite the car wasn't it."

"Aye," Kaylie said. "I loved that car."

"Do you remember who you sold it to?"

Now the woman's back straightened. "No, I don't think so."

"Oh, I know that you do," Liz leaned forward. It was easy for Bernie to forget that Liz could be quite intimidating with her sharp suit and her even sharper mind.

"We had a little chat with your pal Perrie Mellworth. Wasn't it generous of you to give her your car."

A pink flush had appeared in Kaylie's cheeks. "Oh, yes, I guess it was. I couldn't afford to run it, but Perrie could."

"Funny that you would just give it to her. I mean, it wasn't a cheap car."

"I think she paid me something for it," Kaylie said. "It was a long time ago and I can't really remember."

"It should stick out in your mind. It was the day after your boyfriend was killed."

Liz's words rang out in the room like a gunshot.

"I told you I don't like to talk about it. It was very traumatic for me."

Liz pulled out her phone. "That's right you've said. But here's the thing. Perrie was good enough to give us access to her bank records. I told her that the police would take into account the fact that she cooperated with us when it came to sentencing."

"Sentencing for what?"

"Well, I think they call it impeding a police investigation. But you might as well call it what it was. Covering up the fact that you killed Lenny.

"Now I know that you're taking the piss," Kaylie stood up, quivering with rage. Bernie had to admit, she was quite the actress.

"Perrie's bank records show that she didn't pay you anything for the car and that you also transferred ten thousand pounds into her account. All because Perrie did you one little favour, right?"

Kaylie had pressed her lips together, but as Liz and Bernie let the silence lengthen, she couldn't keep quiet any longer.

"Look, it was an accident, all right? I didn't mean to do it."

Liz was reminded of when Isioma spilt a glass of juice or dropped a toy. It was like Kaylie expected them to say: 'oh, I didn't realise it was an accident. It's okay that you killed someone then'.

"What happened?"

"It sounds like you know all about it already," Kaylie said, her tone like a sulky teenager. "I was driving back from the party and Lenny was being an arse, by the way. I'd had two, maybe three big glasses of wine, so I would have been over the limit, but it wasn't like I was falling over drunk or anything. I just wanted to drive so that I could choose the tunes, but Len kept going on about wanting something different. I went to change it on my phone and I don't know, I hit a pothole or something and then…"

Slowly, it seemed to occur to her that she had said too much.

"But it doesn't matter. You're not the police. You can't do anything about it."

"That's right," Bernie nodded. "We're not the cops, and that's why you've got a limited time offer. Unlike the police, we give people a chance. We've already told Perrie to go and hand herself in, and the same offer stands for you. I know you're used to being able to wriggle your way out of trouble, but it's caught up with you now. Do yourself a favour and tell the police everything. They might take it into account when it comes before the judge."

Kaylie looked at them for a moment, then stood up.

"Get out of my flat," she said and they were happy to oblige.

"Reckon she'll hand herself in?" Bernie asked Liz as they walked out to the car.

"Maybe. Want to take a bet on it?"

"No," Bernie replied. "I never gamble."

"You bet me twenty quid that Mary would bang her head in the park the other day."

"That wasn't gambling, that was a sure thing. She always forgets what height she is when she's trying to get her kids off the climbing frame."

Liz gave her a funny look. "Have you ever lost at anything in your life?"

"Never twice," Bernie snapped back. "Now let's get this

meeting written up and close the case. I don't think Kaylie's dad is going to keep paying us now, do you?"

Chapter 30: Liz

Liz found herself on her own outside Ryan Porter's house. Bernie who had been so eager to interview Kaylie had decided she would sit this one out.

"It needs tact," Bernie had told her, with a surprising amount of self-awareness, "and I'll only point out what an idiot he was to fall for Kaylie in the first place."

On reflection, her partner was probably right. From what she'd heard about Ryan he was a nice, if somewhat simple lad. His day was about to get very complicated indeed.

Ryan Porter let her in when she rang the bell so quickly that he might have been waiting behind the door.

"How's things with your mum," Liz asked as she was shown into the kitchen. She knew that she was stalling for time, but she didn't want to send the young lad's world crashing down around him. Not for a couple of minutes at least.

"We're talking again. I mean, I'm still mad at her that she didn't tell me. But I guess she was protecting my relationship with my dad. I saw a video online about how it's, like, super important for men to get on with their fathers. So maybe she was trying to do the right thing? Support the bro-code or something?"

"I understand," Liz said, who wasn't sure if she did or not. But she was pleased that Ryan was at least trying to forgive his mother. As the parent of a teenage son, her worst fear was that one day she would make a mistake bad enough that Sean would stop talking to her.

Ryan scratched the back of his neck. "Can you just let me know now if you found my dad? I don't think I can take not knowing any longer."

"We did," Liz said. "I've got his name and a few pictures of him from social media. He's now known as Martin Gortat and he's based in Nottingham."

She passed a sheaf of printed pages into Ryan's waiting hands.

"He looks like me, doesn't he," Ryan said, staring at the picture of his father like his eyes could burn a hole in it.

"I guess," Liz said, who thought that they both looked like pale, light-haired Caucasian males and anything else was wishful thinking.

"I suppose he'll be a Forrest fan," Ryan said, in a way that was probably meant to mean something but that Liz found baffling. "When do you think I should get in touch with him?"

"Look, this might not go how it does on the telly," Liz warned him. The way he was staring at the photograph of his father with puppy-dog eyes was making her mothering heart ache. "I know you see these long lost family shows and it's all hugs and kisses and stuff. But there's no guarantee that your dad will even be interested in seeing you."

Ryan winced like she had hit him.

"He might be happy about it," Liz said, trying not to crush his spirit. "But I just want you to be prepared that it might not go how you want it to. Remember, he probably doesn't even know that you exist."

"No, he's been living his life with his other family all this time, hasn't he," Ryan said, rubbing his eyes with his sleeve. "I can't thank you enough. I mean, I never thought you would find him."

"You're welcome," Liz said. Despite her reservations, it was truly a pleasure when the job was like this, seeing the genuine relief on Porter's face.

"And now I can tell Kaylie that the wedding is back on."

And then sometimes the job was like walking into the living room and discovering your toddler had crapped on the carpet.

"Ah. About that. There's something you might need to know about Kaylie. I don't think the wedding will be happening anytime soon."

Ryan tore his eyes away from the image of his father. "What, she wants to postpone it?"

"Yeah. Maybe for five to ten years I reckon."

"Sorry, I don't understand."

Liz sighed. "I'm afraid that during our investigations we learned that Kaylie was involved in a crime. She was driving a car that was in a crash and someone was killed. She lied about it to the police and now it's all come out. Right now there's a host of police officers at her house interviewing her, and I reckon she'll be in custody by this evening."

Ryan Porter just stared straight ahead. He gave his head a little shake, like he was trying to dislodge this new idea from his brain.

"That can't be true."

"It is."

"Well then… Well, I'm going to marry her anyway. I'll stand by her. I'm not going to abandon her in her hour of need. What sort of boyfriend would I be if I did that?"

Time for some tough love, Liz thought. "Maybe I should tell you exactly what she did to her last boyfriend."

Fifteen minutes later they heard a key in the lock.

"Oh bloody hell, that'll be mum," Ryan said, wiping his eyes. He looked like he'd spent the afternoon with Mike Tyson, his face so swollen and blotchy from crying.

It only took Mrs Porter a minute to realise that something was wrong.

"What the hell have you been doing to upset my lad," she said, dropping the shopping bags she'd been hauling into the kitchen.

"I'm afraid Ryan has had some bad news, Mrs Porter," Liz told her.

"About… about his dad?"

"Not exactly."

Ryan lifted his head from his arms. "It's Kaylie, mum. Turns out she… she wasn't who I thought she was at all."

Mrs Porter looked at Liz and there was a glint in her eyes.

"The wedding's off then?"

"Yes."

"Good. I know you loved her, but she was never good enough for you. And I'm not just saying that as your mum. That girl was only interested in herself."

Liz grabbed her coat and showed herself out of the house. It was funny how often mums turned out to be right, even if it was for the wrong reasons. She was sure that Mrs Porter would enjoy hearing the story of why Kaylie would no longer be in their lives. And maybe she would be thinking that Ryan had made a lucky escape in the end. What was a little heartache compared to being killed, then abandoned like a piece of rubbish. He had lost a fiancée but he might just have gained a father. Liz just had to hope that the exchange would prove to be worth it in the end.

Chapter 31: Walker

The first briefing in the newly relocated incident room was going better than Walker had expected. For one thing, everyone had access to the desks and computers that had been missing at the conference venue. And for another, DCI Allen had found some decent coffee. She wasn't sharing it around, but even the smell of it was keeping everyone awake, even though it was well past knocking-off time.

Walker had already downed some painkillers to deal with his thumping head. He had spent the last couple of hours going through Tiana's phone, trying to find out if there was any link to whoever killed her. The techs had taken until now to get all the social media apps opened up without passwords, but the hoped-for evidence hadn't materialised so far. He had checked every email and message account she had and it was clear that Tiana herself had never been a target of Fletcher Moon's threatening letters. This backed up what the actor had said in the interview room, so although he had been charged with endangerment of life and a host of other minor offences related to the letters, they had had to release him as a suspect in the murder case.

Mary's observation that Anetta had lied about the last time she had seen Tiana was an interesting one, but when questioned the actress had simply claimed that she 'forgot'. Without any reason to suspect that Anetta had a motive for Tiana's death, it was simply another dead end.

It was a welcome distraction when the DCI called for their attention at the smartboard.

"I've just had a message from Professor Rankin," she said to the half dozen officers who hadn't slunk off for the day. "It says here that someone asked for Tiana's toxicology screen to be expedited, with special attention to any signs of drug use or alcohol in the blood."

Walker coughed and raised his hand. "That was me. It was something that the producer, Tony Ashley said. He thought that Tiana had been drinking, but no one else had mentioned it. He said that her speech was slurred and she was unsteady on her feet. So I wanted to see if he was just trying to put us off or if there was something in it."

"I'm not sure whether to be irritated you didn't tell me or pleased you took the initiative," the Chief Inspector said. Walker decided it was best to say nothing at this point.

"The Professor has sent in the results," Allen continued. "In fact, she even deigned to take time out of her busy schedule to call me directly. Tiana Schmidt's blood showed no trace of alcohol, but there was a significant amount of Ketamine."

This was greeted with incredulous murmurs by her audience.

"Woah, we had no idea she was a drug user, did we?" Macleod asked.

"No. Ketamine is used recreationally, of course, but there was nothing else in her system like opioids that she might have taken with it. It's pretty unusual for someone to just do K on its own like that. Usually it's at least taken with alcohol, but like I said she was clear."

"We need to talk to her friends again," Walker said. "Find out if this was a usual thing."

"Could it have been the cause of death?" Macleod asked.

"Rankin wouldn't rule out that the ketamine played a part. Mind you, the woman doesn't rule anything out so that's not saying much. The most she'll go for is 'improbable'. Apparently death from ketamine overdose is pretty rare. The head wound is the more likely suspect. Although it explains the lack of blood. Something to do with ketamine's effect on the blood clotting process, it's all in the file that the Professor sent over."

While it was nice to have that particular mystery solved, Walker couldn't help but feel that the tox screen had provided more questions than answers.

"So Tony Ashley was telling the truth about what he saw," Walker said, talking it through. "Only what he thought was alcohol intoxication was actually the effects of the anaesthetic drug."

DCI Allen sighed. "It's muddied the waters, that's for sure, but at least it gives us a lead to track down. Find out where she got the Ket and who supplied it to her. If she's got herself involved with some nasty characters from the drugs scene, it could explain why she was killed."

"I don't know, boss," Macleod replied. "I mean, this is a nice wee American lassie looking for a small amount of recreational drugs. I can't see her annoying any of the drugs gangs enough for them to call this much attention on themselves."

"And I've just been through her phone records," Walker added. "She could have deleted messages, of course, but there nothing to suggest she was arranging to get high."

"Don't rain on my parade before it's even started," Allen warned them. "Unless you've got any better leads I want you to put all your efforts into this drugs angle."

Macleod checked his watch. "Better make it tomorrow though boss. We're all walking dead here right now."

"Fine, I can't afford the overtime anyway," Allen replied. "Get a few hours sleep and I'll see you back here for the morning shift. I reckon we're going to crack this thing tomorrow."

They filtered out of the room and Walker wasn't sure if she was trying to convince the troops, or herself.

"Want a lift home?" Rav asked him.

"Aye, thanks."

"Your place or the girlfriend's?"

"Mine. When I'm home late I don't go to hers. It's not fair to wake the kids up."

"You're a good bloke," Rav slapped him on the back. Walker nodded, not sure if the words were sincere or not. When they had first met, Rav had made several comments suggesting that

Mary Plunkett was some sort of gold-digger figure. Which if he had known her for two seconds he would have understood was patently absurd. The closest she had come was singing the song and doing both the Kanye and Jamie Foxx parts.

Rav must have noticed he'd gone quiet, because he started to explain himself.

"Nah, I'm not taking the piss. I know that you're into all that found-family stuff. I didn't really get it but then I was watching this movie the other day where this guy gets this weirdo son and even though he's totally rubbish, he learns that he sort of loves being a dad. And there's a dead duck."

Walker stopped in his tracks. "Are you talking about *About a Boy*?"

"That's it."

"I'm hardly Hugh bloody Grant."

"That's not what I'm trying to say. It's like, my mum's always going on about me getting married, right? Like she's dying for grandkids. But I've no interest in it. I like my life just as it is. And if I can know that my mum's talking bullshit when she says I should settle down and get married, then it makes sense that you would know the opposite. Like, maybe you like kids in the same way that I can't stand them."

"You know, that almost made sense," Walker told him.

"Aye. And I saw that picture of Mary dressed up as a sexy fairy for Halloween and she was well fit."

This was less pleasing. "Right. She wasn't a sexy fairy, by the way. She was Arwen from Lord of the Rings."

"Exactly. You two are made for each other."

"On this one, I'll agree with you."

Chapter 32: Mary

As soon as the kids were dropped off at school on Wednesday morning Mary headed over to WWC headquarters. She had brought with her a selection of cream cakes from the bakers as they had decided to have a bit of a celebration.

"It's a pity it's too early for champagne," Liz said as she opened up the box of cakes and selected a chocolate doughnut.

"But not too early for refined sugar, I see," Bernie said, although Mary knew she was secretly pleased. Mary had brought her a charcuterie platter and a fruit plate instead, and the woman was tucking in quite happily.

"I just wish we were having the same success with the Tiana Schmidt case that Liz had with Lenny Ingot," Bernie said.

"Yeah, you really bossed that one," Mary told her.

"Just doing my job," Liz replied, but Mary could tell she was pleased.

"And I've got some news from Walker on the Schmidt case, although I'm not sure it makes much sense. He was telling me that the pathologist did some sort of blood screening on Tiana and it came back positive for Ketamine."

Bernie whistled. "Now that is a surprise."

"I know. Tony Ashley saw her stumbling and speaking slowly and thought she was drunk. It's weird though, because I saw her not long before that and she was totally fine."

"Huh." Liz brushed some sugar off her top. "Do the cops have any explanation for it?"

"Just that she must have been taking it recreationally, but I'm not too sure. I mean, I know you can't always tell, but she didn't seem the type somehow. Plus she put up all this anti-drug stuff after the Charles Midhurst thing."

"Who's Charles Midhurst?" Bernie asked.

Sometimes Mary forgot that her friends weren't steeped in *Vampyra* lore. "Oh, it's such a sad story. It was all over the forums at the time. Midhurst was this young guy who worked on the show. Something low level, like a personal assistant I think. He was only just out of college, but he got mixed up in drugs and he died from a heroin overdose."

"He died? While he was working on the show?"

"Yeah. He hadn't been there long."

Bernie had pursed her lips. "You didn't think to mention that someone else from *Vampyra* died while working on the show?"

Mary flinched. "Well, I didn't even connect them. I mean, it was two years ago for a start. Maybe three. And he had only worked on the show for a couple of weeks. The cast put up an in memoriam post on their website, but you got the feeling that none of them really knew him. If you think about it hundreds of people work on these sorts of shows. Thousands probably if you count all the backstage stuff. I just never connected it with Tiana."

"But you said she had posted about him?"

Now Mary was feeling like maybe she had missed something. "Yeah. I suppose I should have remembered. But again, it was a kind of generic thing like, isn't it sad how drugs take away young lives, that sort of thing."

Bernie clicked her tongue against the roof of her mouth in disgust.

"Crap," Mary said slowly. "I think you could be right. What if there is a connection. What if there's a drug problem with the crew of *Vampyra*? Could Tiana have been involved somehow"

"I don't know," Liz said, always the rational one. "Ketamine and heroin are kind of on different ends of the scale."

"True, but there's often one thing in common with different drugs," Bernie said. "The person supplying them. What if the same person supplied Charles Midhurst and Tiana Schmidt?"

Mary still couldn't reconcile the idea of Tiana as a drug user. She had seemed so passionate about the victims of drug addiction in her social media. What if something else was going on?

"Hang on," Mary said, the idea clarifying in her mind. "What's the one thing we know about Tiana?"

Liz shook her head. "I'm not sure what you mean."

"She was a whistle-blower," Mary said, her voice getting higher with excitement. "She didn't put up with anyone's crap. We saw that with how she outed Moon as a racist. I reckon this is the same thing. Tiana couldn't just stand by and let that sort of behaviour slide. What if she was going to do the same thing, only this time the target was whoever was supplying the drugs."

They looked at each other for a moment.

"I think you might have something there," Liz said slowly. "If we agree that Tiana wasn't the sort of person to take drugs willingly. But what if she threatened someone and they drugged her without her knowledge."

"I don't know, it seems a little overly complicated," Bernie said.

"No, I like this idea," Mary insisted, not willing to let Bernie rain on her parade. "Tiana confronts the dealer and they fight back by putting the ketamine in her drink."

"And then they hit her over the head just to make sure?" Bernie pointed out. "You've got something there, Mary, but I'm not sure it quite fits."

"I know I'm right," Mary said stubbornly. "I'm just not sure how I'm going to prove it."

"I don't know either," Liz said slowly. "We need some real evidence, or a confession and if the killer has got away with it for this long they're not exactly going to break down and confess. I don't think this is a case where we can just send Bernie in to shout at someone. We're going to have to be more subtle than that."

"Then it's over to you two," Bernie said. "But need I remind you that in all of this, all you've identified is a motive. We need a suspect first."

Mary thought back to Anetta's lies about Tiana doing her make-up. "Do you know what, I might just know where to start looking."

Chapter 33: Bernie

If I never hear another word about vampires or dragons, Bernie Paterson thought, then it will be too soon. The official WWC meeting on Wednesday morning had broken up when Liz had left, claiming she needed to watch Isioma when Dave went to work. Bernie reckoned she just wanted to get away from Mary and her endless theories about the drug scene among the *Vampyra* set. She had fixated on Anetta at first, until Bernie pointed out that the woman seemed to have no motive to kill her make-up artist. Now she was just accusing random cast members.

"I mean, Alderick is pretty skinny," Mary was saying while she nibbled at what Bernie reckoned was at least her fourth cream cake. "He could be doing all sorts of diet pills."

"Because that's the same as heroin," Bernie muttered, but the other woman pretended not to hear her.

"And Tony Ashley was quick to point the finger at other people, wasn't he? What if it went right to the top."

Bernie was growing tired of this. "Liz said that Ashley made seven million dollars from his last movie. I'm not sure he has to do some dealing on the side."

"True."

"Let's think it through," Bernie told her. "I don't see why the dealer responsible for Charles Midhurst's death has to be a member of the cast. It could be literally anyone, right? Didn't you say Midhurst died out on California?"

"Yeah. On that season they filmed half in Hollywood, half in Scotland."

"Then surely the person responsible is some Californian drug pusher? And I don't see how we'll track them down."

Mary went quiet for a bit. Bernie took the opportunity to do some press-ups. She was missing one of her gym sessions to listen to her friend's blather.

A ringing phone made her jump. "Get it will you?" she called to Mary, not wanting to stop mid-press.

"It's only Liz anyway," Mary told her. Bernie puffed out her last set of twenty and got back up off the floor just as Mary was ending the call.

"What was that about?"

Mary looked smug. "On her way back to the house Liz put in a call with Alderick. Do you remember how he went back to the States already? Well, there's no love lost between him and Anetta, we know that already. I'd go as far as to say she hates his guts."

"And?"

"Liz told Alderick that the case was going so slowly that he might have to get on a plane back to Scotland, unless he could tell us something about Anetta. Maybe some sort of connection to drugs. And he came through big time.

Apparently it's fairly well known that Anetta has a major coke habit."

"That's good," Bernie said. "It supports your theory that there's a drug connection here. But we're not thinking that Anetta's dealing, right? So assuming that the dealer is who killed Tiana to keep her silence, we've still got a mysterious drug pusher that we can't pin down. And like I said, there's no reason to believe they're part of the *Vampyra* cast or crew."

"Do you know what, I think I might have worked it out," Mary said, straightening up in her chair. "Here's the thing, I was just thinking about season two. They filmed the whole thing in Singapore, in a skyscraper there. It was meant to look all futuristic for the part that shows the dragons living in space."

"Hang on, there's a season set in space?" Bernie was finding the inconsistencies with this dreadful series disorientating. "What the hell kind of show is this?"

"I'll lend you the DVDs later," Mary said quickly. "Look, my point is this was during covid. It was a closed set with only the actors and crew allowed to socialise with each other. If Anetta had the sort of drug habit that she has now, then where was she getting it from? Even without the pandemic protocols, Singapore isn't exactly drug-friendly."

Bernie was starting to understand where Mary was coming from. "You think her supplier was part of the cast, then? Or a crew member."

"I can't see how she would have access to it otherwise. I reckon her dealer was part of the *Vampyra* family."

Despite her initial scepticism, Bernie was starting to be won around. "All right, let's be clear I understand what's happening here. Tiana is a whistleblower who doesn't stand for any crap on set. She finds out that one of the crew or the actors was responsible for the drugs that led to Charles Midhurst's death. And she decided to take them down somehow? Only before that happened, they killed her."

"And that's why the ketamine was found in her system, even though she was anti-drugs," Mary said, her voice triumphant.

"But it wasn't the ketamine that killed Tiana," Bernie reminded her. "It was a blow to the head."

"I know, and I can't explain that one yet. But it's still the best theory we've got."

"And better than anything the coppers have come up with," Bernie agreed. "Okay, you've convinced me. What next?"

"We tell the police. And then we go and speak to Anetta. She's the only one we know for sure was involved in the drugs side. If she's not the dealer, then she must know who is."

"Got it."

"I'll just grab one more apple turnover for the road."

Chapter 34: Liz

When Bernie popped into her house to say that she and Mary were going to Glasgow and could she do some digging into Anetta's finances, Liz had only one response.

"No."

Bernie had goggled at her. "What the hell do you mean, no?"

"I mean no. This time I want to be in on the murder investigation. I want to be involved, not just sat on the laptop doing the research."

Liz folded her arms and planted her feet apart. Unless Bernie was prepared to wrestle her to the ground – and let's face it, that wasn't totally out of the question – she wasn't changing her mind.

"Fine," Bernie moaned. "You can sit in the front with me. Mary is sulking because she had to ask her ex to watch the kids."

"My mum's away," Mary explained when they were all in the car. "And I've used up my babysitting credits with everyone else. Matt's in the area for a work thing so I've asked him to step in after school."

"Well, that's good isn't it?"

"Yeah, only now I owe him a favour. He'll probably make me take another one of Stephanie's online yoga classes. Last time

I thought I was safe because I said my camera wasn't working. Only Peter came in and turned it one halfway through."

"Let me guess," Liz smiled. "You weren't doing the yoga?"

"I was eating a pop tart on the sofa. It was mortifying."

Liz couldn't stop a laugh bubbling up at that one, but one of the good things about Mary was that she was always more than happy to laugh at herself.

"I know, I'm ridiculous."

"I just hope this drug dealer theory of yours isn't ridiculous too," Bernie told her. "Tell Liz what Macleod said when we told him about it."

"He said it was all very well for 'us lot' to have wild theories, but the police need evidence first. Which is fair enough, to be honest. He's let Walker come over and meet us, just in case we do get somewhere today."

"Aye, he'll be happy enough to take the credit if we break the case," Bernie snapped.

"True."

They pulled into the parking lot of the conference centre and found a space.

"We better solve this case soon," Bernie grumbled. "These parking charges are playing havoc with our expenses for the month."

Probably best that Bernie didn't know that Mary had been

adding all the coffees and pastries she'd had that week to the WWC expenses document, Liz thought. She would let that bombshell hit at the end of the month.

They made their way to the hotel and slipped past Reception when the man behind the desk was busy. While they were walking up the stairs, Mary rummaged in her bag and brought out a plastic container full of pre-prepared fruit.

"Anetta's from California, right?" Mary explained when she saw Liz's confused face. "When I grabbed the stuff for our wee celebration this morning I picked her up a tropical fruit platter. Thought it might be a nice bit of bribery."

"A bag of cocaine might have gone down better," Bernie quipped.

"Well, I wasn't going to get that in M&S, was I?"

Bernie led the way up to Anetta's room. They knocked on the door and the actress answered after a few minutes. This was the first time Liz had seen her in the flesh and she was just as beautiful as she was on screen. Her skin was flawless and Liz was dying to ask her what products she used, but it didn't feel like the right time.

"We wanted to ask you a couple more questions," Bernie told her.

"There's a surprise."

Mary scooted forward and held out her prize. "And we brought you this."

"You brought me some fruit? It's not a sex thing, is it? Like an upside-down pineapple."

"Oh god no," Mary flapped her hands in distress. "I just thought, seeing as you were from California that you might be finding our diet a wee bit stodgy. And you might like something lighter."

Anetta tapped her toe on the ground. "Well, you're not wrong. Tell me, why does every meal in Scotland contain bread of some description?"

"You're telling me," Bernie grinned, delighted to find a kindred spirit. "You should hear the amount of refined carbs people eat here."

"And sulphites?" Anetta asked her.

"They don't even know what sulphites are."

"You're kidding me." The actress took a hungry look at the fruit. "Oh, I suppose you could come in. But you've only got ten minutes. I'm going out for a facial this afternoon."

Anetta sat in a chair with her fruit plate and a plastic fork while the other three squeezed onto a sofa together. Liz hated sitting so close to Bernie: the woman was all elbows.

"Well, what is it you want now?"

"You seem a little tense," Bernie told her.

"Tense? I'm goddamn pissed off. I'm meant to be starting this new play soon. I've already missed one full cast rehearsal."

"Are you worried they'll give the part to someone else?"

Anetta flicked her hair over her shoulder. "If they do they'll have to refund a hell of a lot of tickets. It's only having my name on the bill that's got them this far."

Mary was playing good cop this time, so she leaned forward to speak to Anetta. "We thought you might be pleased to hear that Fletcher Moon has been arrested for sabotaging the lighting rig. And for sending the threatening letters to yourself and other members of the cast."

"The little weasel," Anetta said. "Although I can't say that I'm surprised."

"You knew that he'd fallen out with Tiana?"

"He came onto her."

"And called her racist names."

Anetta curled her lip. "I hadn't heard that bit. But again, not a surprise."

"Tiana wasn't the sort of person to let things like that go."

"Good for her," Anetta said, but her attention was on the piece of strawberry she had speared with a fork. "So that's why he killed her then?"

"Actually, we don't think that Moon killed her. He sent the letters, and he damaged the stage, but he wasn't a killer."

"I suppose he told you that and you believed him?"

"It's more that the police found something new," Liz said. "They got the toxicology result on Tiana's blood."

The way that Anetta's shoulders twitched was almost a confession. The woman kept her head down and didn't say a word.

"It turns out that there was a significant amount of ketamine in her system."

"Huh."

Mary took up the questioning. "I was at the panel that day. And the thing is, I know you were lying when you said you hadn't seen Tiana before the panel. She had done your tattoo art before you went on stage."

Anetta curled her upper lip. "You're right, I forgot about that. But I'm telling you that she was still one hundred per cent alive when I left her."

"But not a hundred per cent sober," Bernie said. "Because you slipped her the drugs, didn't you?"

"Why would I do something like that?"

"Tiana wasn't afraid to take people down if she felt they were in the wrong. And we think it came back to Charles Midhurst."

"The kid that died?"

"Yeah. From an overdose."

Anetta narrowed her eyes. "Look, I've got nothing to do with the hard stuff. Just the usual things to get you through those boring Hollywood parties. I never even met Midhurst."

"But you did put the ketamine in Tiana's drink, didn't you," Liz prompted. "And if you won't talk to us about it we're going to get the police detectives over here. Maybe they'll search this room. Do you think they'll find anything incriminating?"

"You can't... they would need a warrant."

"Ah, but you let us in," Bernie told her. "And look at that spoon you've got there on the table. Probably drug paraphernalia, right?"

"Oh come on, you just watched me scoop a blueberry with it."

The three women kept their mouths shut.

"Fine," Anetta let her perfect posture slump. "I put the stuff in her drink. But she was the one threatening me. She caught me in the ladies loos. I hadn't locked the stall and I was taking a little pick-me-up for the panel. God, those things are boring. Anyway, rather than just pretending she hadn't seen anything, she totally went off on one. Saying that I should know better and that maybe I had had something to do with the kid's overdose. All total crap. But she said that she was going to bad-mouth me all over town. That I would never get another job. You all think she was so great, but she could be a nasty bitch when she wanted to."

"And that's when you decided to kill her."

"Not kill her. Just show her up a little. I guess I thought

maybe she would make a fool of herself, people would think she was a user… I wasn't really thinking at all. I just wanted her to get sacked or something. If she made an ass of herself then she would be off the set. I knew Tony was only looking for a reason to get rid of her. He was already pissed that she had made such a fuss about that dick Fletcher Moon."

"Tony told us he had supported Tiana."

Anetta laughed. "Yeah, right. Supported her so that it was all dealt with as quickly and as quietly as possible, more like. Look, there are two types of men in this industry. The a-holes that feel you up and the so-called 'good guys' who never touch you but spend all their time covering up for the other ones."

This was a grim view of the entertainment industry, but the *Vampyra* situation seemed to back it up at least.

"Didn't you think you should support Tiana instead of trying to take her down?"

"Come on, don't be so naïve," Anetta snapped. "She was on a crusade. Take down the evil drug lords or whatever. She didn't consider that most of us were just having a bit of fun. And it was so freaking patronising. The way she told me I should give up for my own good. Like, please shut your mouth."

That would be a no then.

"I'd got a little bit of K just to help me to sleep at night. Combine it with a couple of vodkas and I'm out like a light. She had this stupid massive cup of coffee and when she went to the loo, I popped a couple of tablets in there. I never thought... it was like a prank, you know?"

Liz was reminded of Kaylie Michelson saying that Lenny's death was just an accident. Some people never learned to take responsibility for their actions.

"And then you went backstage and thumped her over the back of the head, just to make sure," Bernie said.

"What?" Anetta pressed her knees together. "No, I couldn't do something like that. She must have fallen over or something. I mean, I didn't know the drugs would kill her, did I? I just wanted to humiliate her. Teach her a lesson."

"Are you going to tell us that you poisoned Tiana but you didn't actually bash her head in?"

"If someone killed her by hitting her on the head, then it wasn't me." Anetta blinked, then raised a hand to her chest. "Oh thank god, it wasn't me. Someone else killed her after the ketamine. Wow. I thought I'd totally ruined my career."

"And killed someone."

"Yeah, that too." Her body actually sagged with relief. Until that moment Liz hadn't believed she was innocent, but no one could fake that sort of physical response.

The members of the WWC exchanged bewildered looks. The idiot actress had drugged Tiana without her knowledge, but that was the extent of her crimes. They were going to have to look elsewhere for her killer.

"Look, we're going to have to tell the police about your assault on Tiana."

"It was hardly that," Anetta sniffed. Since learning that she wasn't a murderer the woman had regained her uptight composure. "Just a prank, like I said."

"Listen, you need to wise up here," Bernie told her. "The police are going to be all over you because of the ketamine. The only way to get them off your back is if you tell us who was getting you the drugs."

"It was just a little something to keep me going. You Scots are so puritanical."

"Nah, we're Calvinists, not Puritans," Mary told her, "same result really, but a different name."

Anetta looked confused and Liz tried to keep them on topic.

"It might have just been recreational for you, but it didn't end up that way for Charles Midhurst. You know how annoyed Tiana got with you about the drugs. Don't you think she would have confronted the dealer too? If there is a connection between Midhurst's death and Tiana's, then it won't look good for you if you try and protect that person."

"Fine," Anetta said, rolling her eyes. "It's not as if I even like the guy. And he can't write decent dialogue to save his life."

Chapter 35: Walker

Walker was feeling seriously outnumbered. Not only was he sitting with two superior officers, Macleod and DCI Allen, but on the other side of the conference table the entirety of the WWC was staring him down.

"This is all theoretical," DCI Allen said once the ladies had explained what they believed had happened to Tiana Schmidt. "And Anetta Strong's testimony is going to be largely hearsay."

"True," Mary said. Walker had the feeling that the others had nominated her to take the lead in this meeting. This was mainly based on the fact that Liz kept elbowing Bernie in the ribs each time she tried to speak.

"We've sent Sergeant Sangar and his team over to Anetta's hotel room," DCI Allen continued. "So thank you for the information. If we find the ketamine then we can arrest her for spiking Tiana's drink. That'll get her time to question her over the murder."

"She didn't know about the head wound," Mary told them. "I don't think she was responsible for it."

"Well, I'm afraid we can't take that chance. We'll question her under caution."

Mary nodded. "That's what we thought you would say. But our worry is that the dealer will notice her being taken away in a police car. He's staying at the same hotel after all. And he's obviously got contacts."

"You think he's a flight risk?"

"Yes."

DCI Allen tapped her fingertips on the table. "I see. What do you propose?"

Mary took the lead once more. "We would like to interview him, alongside your officers. Tell him that you're arresting Anetta and that we know about the doping. And then see where it goes."

"You reckon you can what… sweet talk him into confessing?" Allen asked.

Walker cleared his throat. "You'd be surprised at how often it works."

The DCI pinched the bridge of her nose. "You understand the risks for me? If it goes wrong then the press will be all over it. A bunch of amateurs leading an interview –" she broke off to shake her head in despair.

"I understand completely. That's why we won't be leading it. I'll be there because I was a witness to what happened to Tiana. It'll be your men that lead the interview, I'll just be there to make him think that there's no reason to panic."

"And what are the other two, your support animals?"

Ouch, Walker thought, making sure not to look at Bernie after that one.

"Look, you know you don't have the evidence to arrest him," Liz said, taking up the narrative. "If we frame it as an informal chat, just a search for information with a nerdy fan on hand, then we might just get him to agree to talk to us."

DCI Allen looked to Macleod. "You've used them before?"

"Yes," Macleod nodded. "We've had the WWC as consultants on a few cases. They've never let us down."

"Then I hold you directly accountable if the whole thing ends up in a big steaming heap of crap."

With that ringing endorsement, Walker, Macleod and the women from the WWC made their way over to the conference centre. In separate cars, so that no one murdered each other before they even got started.

Tim Errin might have been in the same hotel as Anetta and the others, but his position in the cast was clear as he had a small standard room on the ground floor. Because the idea of them all squeezing into the room with him might not exactly put the man at his ease, Mary asked him to join them in the bar area.

Walker was thankful that his current status as a trainee detective meant he was in a suit. He reckoned that Errin would have fled if he had seen a police uniform. The writer had the look of a nervous man who was trying not to seem nervous. He had his hands in his pockets but was chewing on the inside of his cheek.

"Mr Errin, thank you for agreeing to meet with us," Macleod said. "I don't know if you've heard, but we've arrested Anetta

Strong. She admitted putting Ketamine in Tiana's coffee."

Tim Errin looked shocked. "God, I can't believe she did that. I mean, I guess I knew she was sort of ruthless, but to think she would take it that far. Poor Tiana."

"We wanted to inform everyone on the panel personally," Mary said. "I was there you see, in the audience. I know how traumatic it all was."

Tim bowed his head. "It was awful. I mean, when the lighting rig went down we thought it was some sort of terrorist thing. I've lived in the US for years now, and mostly in gun-happy states, but that's the most scared I've ever been."

"And no one realised that Tiana had been hurt," Walker prompted.

"No. And now you're saying that Anetta did it?"

That wasn't what they were saying at all, and Walker had the feeling that Errin knew that fine well.

"Like the Inspector said, she admitted to spiking the drink."

"I never thought she would go that far," Errin said. "I mean, she could be a pain to work with, but this is another level."

"You never liked Anetta, then?" Walker prompted.

"I guess we always tried to keep on her good side," Errin gave them a nervous smile. "As the writers we just provide the words, you know? The star is the important one. That kind of diva image, well, it has its roots in truth doesn't it."

"Anetta was a diva?"

"Right," he nodded. "She could be difficult, for sure. If you didn't give her enough lines, or ensure that she was in the most scenes, then she would kick off. I know one time she stormed into the writers' room because Alderick had ended up with more screentime that episode. Like I said, I'm not surprised that she went after Tiana if she thought that she'd been crossed, but I can't believe that she killed her."

"Yeah, we don't think she killed her either."

Errin blinked. "Sorry, I thought you just said that you had arrested her for murder?"

"Not exactly. It turns out that Anetta had poisoned Tiana, but someone else killed her. It wasn't Anetta that actually caused her death."

"Wow. So I guess you guys are back to square one. The psycho-killer theory, isn't that right?"

Walker kept his face open and relaxed. "No, I think we're looking a little closer to home."

"What... what do you mean by that?"

It was Mary's voice that came next. "What happened to Charles Midhurst?"

There it was, the sheer panic flashed across the writer's face. If he'd been a bird, he'd have taken off to the sky in a cloud of feathers. As it was, you could see him fighting the urge to jump out of his chair and run from the room.

"That was the poor kid who died, right?"

"Yeah. Did you know him?" Macleod asked.

"Not really. He'd not been there for long."

"You didn't have any contact with him regarding certain transactions, did you?" Liz asked him.

Now Errin's eyes flicked from one person to the next. "What do you mean?"

"When we arrested Anetta we asked who her supplier was. She said that was you."

"God, I knew she would say something like that. It's her that was dealing. She even sold me the odd joint. Look, you can't listen to her. She's one of those narcissists, always changing the story so that she's the victim."

"She could be," Walker nodded. "But Anetta also handed over her phone. And we've only had a chance to look through a few of the messages, but it does seem as if you were her supplier."

Tim Errin was still trying to style it out. "All right, look, I might have passed some stuff on, only when I had a little extra left over. I'm no Walter White."

"Of course not," Mary offered him a little laugh. "You were just trying to help out your friends, right?"

"Exactly."

"Was Tiana your friend?" Mary asked softly, and it was only

because Walker knew her so well that he could hear the undertone of anger in her voice.

He shrugged. "I didn't know her well, but sure, we were friendly."

"Did I mention that our tech department got into Tiana's phone," Walker told him. "There were plenty of messages back and forth between the two of you, sharing memes, moaning about the actors on set, all that sort of stuff. Except for the last week where there was nothing."

Errin just shrugged.

"We were thinking that maybe she found out something about you," Mary told him. "Something that she didn't like."

"That sounds like you're guessing," Errin replied.

"It was enough to get the Justice of the Peace to issue us a warrant."

"What?"

Walker leaned forward. "While you're talking to us right now, we've got a bunch of constables taking apart your hotel room. Here's the warrant if you want to check it's all in order."

He shrugged. "You won't find anything."

"Because you've got rid of everything. Flushed it probably, but we will be checking the drains. Oh, and the warrant also covers your phone."

"Fine," he said, although he definitely looked less pleased at this one.

"We found something else on Tiana's phone," Walker said. "On Saturday she made a call to California."

"That's not surprising, right?"

"No, but the number was. When we looked it up it was the local office for the Los Angeles County Sheriff's Department. On our way over here we called them ourselves. It turned out that she was phoning to find out exactly when Charles Midhurst died. I think she wanted to place you with him when he bought the drugs that killed him."

"She was delusional."

Walker hissed in a breath as the energy in the room changed.

"Tiana did ask you about it, then?"

"Sure she did. She damn well cornered me. Going on and on about Charles Midhurst, like he was her long lost brother or something. She barely even knew the guy. Look, I don't like to speak ill of the dead, but Tiana was basically harassing me."

"Was she now?" Bernie's voice was dangerously low.

"I know what it sounds like, but between Tiana and Anetta it was like twin crazy people."

"Why don't you explain it to us," Mary suggested.

"It was all Anetta's fault. Like I said, she's a narcissist. She told Tiana that I had been at the same party with Charles just before he died. And because of that, Tiana was convinced that

I'd sold him the stuff that he overdosed on."

"You were never interviewed by the police about Midhurst's death?"

"Oh, you're not implicating me in that one. No way. Look, I might pass on a little blow when I can, but I never touch the hard stuff. Wherever Chuck got it from, it wasn't me."

"But Tiana wouldn't listen to that, right?"

The writer was wringing his hands together, his knuckles threatening to poke through the skin. "It was like a crusade or something. She said that the drug scene in *Vampyra* was toxic. That the whole situation needed to be changed. And she was going to tell the producers that I was a part of it. I was begging her not to get me fired. I mean, I need this job. It's my first writing credit and my whole reputation is hanging on it. If it got around that I was dealing then I would never get a job again."

"And that's why you went to see her, right?"

"Exactly," he said, his knee jiggling with adrenaline. "Just to talk to her. I mean, she'd been so friendly to me on the panel, so I thought she would be reasonable. But it was like a switch had flicked. She kept going on about Charles Midhurst, like the idiot kid dying was my fault."

"Wasn't it?"

"No! I didn't give him the smack. I'm strictly weed and pills. But she kept saying that one thing led to another. God, she made me out to be the devil himself."

There wasn't much sympathy in the room by this point.

"I think you had better come down to the station with us so we can interview you under caution," Macleod told him.

"No, that makes me sound guilty. Like it was my fault. But it was Tiana's. She just couldn't let the drugs thing go. Have you any idea how little the writers get paid? I mean, we're barely making more than minimum wage and we're still meant to live in Hollywood with everyone else making huge salaries. I didn't have any choice but to find a side hustle."

"Let's go now," Walker said.

"You just don't understand," Errin was almost frantic now, his face shiny with sweat. "I had a chance of a new gig, Anetta was going to get me a spot in this theatre thing she was doing. I was finally going to get something better than that fantasy, Lord of the Rings rip-off crap."

Mary gasped at this.

"What, you have to admit *Vampyra* was terrible. But Anetta had a new play starting in the West End and she said we just needed to stop Tiana from ratting us out somehow. The drugs were meant to do it, but I guess Anetta couldn't even do that right, because then Tiana came and found me. And she wasn't making much sense by then, just ranting about Midhurst and I pulled her behind the curtain so no one would see and then she bent over like she was going to be sick and I grabbed my laptop and I…"

There was a long moment of silence, then Macleod's mournful

Highland timbre rang out across the bar.

"You have the right to remain silent..."

It took two more hours before Walker had completed the paperwork on the arrest and both Anetta Strong and Tim Errin were in the custody suite.

"Do you reckon we'll get Anetta for conspiracy?" Rav asked once they had returned to the office.

"Depends. At the moment she's sticking to her story that the doping was just a prank. Errin will have to provide some evidence that they were working together. For the moment it's just his word against hers."

"I think I know which one will look better to the jury," Rav added.

Walker shrugged. In truth, once they had done their part he had never let himself get too concerned with what happened next. That was for others to decide.

"There's some envelopes here for the two of you," a female constable told them. "They look official."

"Exam results," Rav said, although Walker had already worked that out. There were certain things deemed too important to deal with over email, and the result of their final exam was one of those.

Walker took his letter and ripped it open immediately. There was no point prolonging the inevitable.

"Unlucky mate," the constable said, reading the disappointment on his face.

He'd sort of known it of course. But it still hurt to see the score of fifty-seven, just three lousy points off the pass mark of sixty. There in black and white was the evidence of his failure.

"You'll smash it on the resit," Rav said loyally and Walker managed a half-smile.

"Yeah, I know."

"Still crap though mate," Rav added and Walker appreciated the man not sugar-coating his words.

"Thanks. Looks like you did great though," Walker noted the bold lettering that stated Rav had scored in the top ten per cent.

"Yeah, well," Rav shrugged, making Walker feel even worse. Not only had he failed, his failure had sucked the joy out of his friend's success.

"You go out and celebrate for me, okay? I'm going to go and speak to DCI Hunter. It says on the bottom that I'm to call him immediately."

"I'm sure he'll say the same about the resit," Rav replied, although he didn't look certain. They both knew that Hunter had been their toughest tutor at the college and he didn't seem like the kind of guy to reach out with hugs and cups of tea.

In some ways, it was lucky that they had ended up on the case in Govan as Hunter who was head of the teaching staff at

Tulliallan College also did two days a week in the office there. It was still a long, lonely walk to Hunter's room. The students called DCI Hunter the Gladiator, in a TV reference that Mary Plunkett would have appreciated. It was also a reference to his teaching style, which certainly felt like being pummelled with a pugil stick. Walker took a deep breath, reminded himself that he was an adult, not a kid about to get told off by the head teacher, and knocked on the door.

"Come in."

"You wrote on my exam result to come and see you, sir. I thought I better do it immediately."

"I'm glad that you did," Hunter said. "I'm off back to the College tomorrow. Take a seat."

Walker sat down on the hard plastic chair opposite the other man's desk. The whole situation was giving him uncomfortable flashbacks of being called to the Headmaster's office, something that had happened often during his school years.

"I wanted to apologise for my result," Walker said, wanting to get his piece in first before the other man started with the bollocking. "I've never been good at exams, and although I did put a lot of work in, I know I could have done better. If you would consider giving me a resit, I would appreciate a second chance."

"You want this move to the Specialist Crime Division badly, don't you."

"Yes sir. I've been working toward it for a long time now. I've spent most of the last two years seconded to one Major Investigation Team or another. I've learned a lot."

Hunter leaned back in his chair, so that he was literally staring down his nose at Walker.

"Newbies like you do like to waste my time, don't you?"

"Sorry, sir?"

"You didn't read the full instructions before the exam, did you?" Hunter asked him.

"Sir?" Walker wondered what he had got wrong this time.

The other man sighed. "No one ever reads the small print. I've half a mind to put something really nasty in there just to catch everyone out. So you didn't see the part about the pass mark?"

"I know that you needed sixty to pass," Walker replied. "And I didn't make it."

"Aye, and did you read the bit about borderline cases?"

He shook his head.

"Of course you bloody didn't. Well, I hope you'll be more meticulous as a detective."

A tiny spark of hope ignited in Walker's heart. "What do you mean, sir?"

"In borderline cases, like yours, where candidates are just

below the test mark we can take into account other aspects of the course. Assessments from superior officers, paperwork, observations of training exercises. And your on-the-beat assessments in particular were excellent. Some of the highest scores I've ever seen. Taking all the other work into account, it gives you an overall pass."

"You mean?"

"Welcome to the Specialist Crime Division, Detective Sergeant Walker."

Chapter 36: Mary

It was after bedtime on Wednesday night when Mary finally made it back home. She hated missing bedtime with the kids, when they would read books together and have five glorious minutes when they weren't demanding screens and electronic stimulation. Peter was going through a Stephen King phase and they had both agreed to read The Shining together, even though Mary had been skipping bits without telling him. But tonight she had to be content with knowing that her ex-husband was watching the kids while she dealt with the minor matter of bringing a murderer to justice. It was a funny life, if you stopped and thought about it. Funny, but good.

Mary put her key in the door and called her ex-husband's name.

"I'm in here," he said.

When Matt got up from the sofa his hair was sticking up at the back and she knew that he had fallen asleep. She couldn't be annoyed, however. She knew just how tiring the kids could be and he had stepped in at the last minute.

"All sorted?" he asked, as if she'd been doing the shopping not taking down a murderer.

"Yes, we got our guy. Thanks for subbing for me today," Mary added. "I know you've had the kids a lot recently, but it was a great help. Mum would have done it, of course, only she's on this painting holiday to Torremolinos."

"Your mum? Painting? Jesus, she's colourblind isn't she?"

Mary couldn't help but laugh. "You're not wrong. One of her pals was going on this trip where they go out in the Spanish countryside and paint hills or something and Nel thought it would be fun. I reckon there will be more Sangria drinking than watercolours going on."

"Remember that time she tried to help us paint the kids' rooms at the house?"

"Oh god," Mary snorted at the memory. "She chose the most awful colour of mustard yellow and it wasn't until it was on the wall that you pointed it that it looked like a baby's nappy. She sulked for a week."

"Aye, I was right though, wasn't I."

He smiled, showing the dimple in his cheek and Mary had the strangest sensation, like the ghost of love. She had to turn away for a second, it was so strong.

"Well, I better get going," Matt stretched out his back. "Got a long drive up to Aberdeen."

Was he trying to make her feel guilty now?

"Thanks again," Mary said as she walked him out of the door.

"No problem. I won't wake up the kids to say bye. It took me far too long to get them down to sleep. Since when does Johnny need the backlist of Oasis's greatest hits sung to him to go to sleep?"

"He's very invested in the reunion," Mary said with a smile.

"Of course." Matt paused on the doorstep. "There was something I wanted to talk to you about."

Mary's spidey senses flickered. He had the sort of expression she knew well from their children. The one that always preceded a confession like 'sorry mum, you never liked that mug anyway did you?' or 'you might want to check the bath'.

His mouth was pulled down at the corners, but he finally managed to get the words out. "The thing is, I'm getting married. Um, to Stephanie."

"Yes, I know that. You've been engaged for a while."

"Right. Well, we got a great deal on the venue and we're going to do it in March.

"Oh." Somehow a date made it so much more real. "Well, that's great. Stephanie will be pleased."

"Yeah, she's made up. We've booked this posh place, a big country house, two hundred guests, the works."

"Sounds lovely," Mary said, her fake smile firmly in place. "I'm so happy for you."

"Excellent, because Stephanie wanted to do a videocall with you," Matt said, already pulling his phone from his pocket. "And I said that would be fine."

"You said what? Matt, I don't think –"

The phone lit up with Stephanie's face and Matt thrust it

towards her. Mary only had a second to plaster on a smile.

"And there she is. Great news about the wedding," Mary chirped.

"I know! I'm so excited. And it'll be so wonderful having you all there."

"Mm-hmnn," Mary kept the smile going and wondered if she would be able to hide at the back where no one could see her reactions. Surely every person there would know she was Matt's ex. Oh god, would he use the same best man?

"And we're going to all be one family, when you think about it," Stephanie was still talking, her perfect eyebrows trembling with excitement. "The children and you of course. That's why I was so pleased when I had the idea. And Matt thought you would say no!"

"Oh, I'm happy to come," Mary replied. And now that the idea was sinking in, that wasn't a million miles from the truth. Yes, for her personally it would be an awkward, miserable experience, but the kids were going to love it, and that would give her some pleasure at least.

"And you'll have such an important role to play."

"I suppose. The kids will need looking after and –"

"Oh, we'll get someone to help with all that. You'll be needed for your Maid of Honour duties."

"Maid of…" Black spots started to appear in Mary's vision and she clutched at the door frame for support. "You want me to be Maid of Honour?"

"Isn't it just the cleverest thing? We couldn't think who to ask, of course all of my friends are much too young... Oh! Not that I mean you're old or anything."

"Of course not." Mary had turned to face Matt and was giving him a death stare. If the stare didn't do it she had a whole arsenal of knowledge of how to get away with murder. Poison, strangulation, a knife wound somewhere unpleasant... The list was endless.

"My phone's getting low on battery darling," Matt said as he pulled the device from Mary's hand. "Love you." He clicked off the call and Stephanie's face disappeared, leaving only silence behind her.

"Maid of honour. Maid of bloody honour." Mary had rounded on her ex-husband like a tiger who had been locked in with a handler. "Are you taking the absolute piss?"

Matt would have backed up, only he was against the door and there was nowhere for him to go. Despite this, he pressed himself against the door like she was an escaped tiger.

"Sorry! I didn't think she'd actually go through with it. But you know what Stephanie's like when she's got something into her head."

"Honestly, isn't it the whole point of divorce that I don't have to deal with this sort of crap anymore. It never occurred to you to just stand up to her?"

He gave her a sort of hopeless shrug.

"Sorry?" He said again, but Mary realised that he didn't really mean it. That was the other thing about divorce. He didn't have to care about her feelings anymore. And there was absolutely nothing she could do about it.

"I could say no," Mary said in a soft voice.

"You won't though will you? You were always the nice one."

She thought about that for a moment. Bernie Paterson would have told her just how problematic it was to always be nice. How 'no' was a complete sentence and she shouldn't be a wet lettuce. But the thing was, she wasn't Bernie. Mary thought about her kids' faces, all of them part of the wedding, all in their smartest clothes, happy for their dad and his new life with Stephanie.

"All right, I'll do it. But not because I'm nice," she said, wagging her finger in his face. "Because I'm a bloody good mother."

"Great! I knew I could count on you to –"

"Now get the hell out of my house."

"Understood."

Epilogue: Walker

It had been a funny sort of week for the newly official Detective Sergeant Owen Walker. When he had heard that he had been given a pass for the exam, despite an initial failure, it hadn't quite sunk in. Not even when Rav took him out for far too many drinks to celebrate. It was only when Mary had squealed with delight and jumped on top of him, followed by all four kids who didn't know what was happening but were always up for a wrestle. Then it had felt real.

The only problem was going to be how to live up to last week. A murder case solved and a move to plain clothes, how could life get any better? Well, here was the thing. Walker had learned early on that if he wanted his life to improve, he had to do it himself. A fairly average, not particularly happy childhood had had one good result which was a tendency to self-reliance. And now that his work was falling into place, it was time to sort out the rest of his life.

It was in that spirit that he had made a visit to a certain little shop at the posh end of Invergryff High Street and made a purchase he had been planning for a long time. Unable to wait a second longer, he drove straight over to Mary's house.

"The kids are out the back," Mary said when he walked in the front door. "I've given them some mentos and a bottle of cola. I figured the rain would wash it all away."

"Sure."

"We're going to have to grab a takeaway for dinner. With the Tiana Schmidt case and everything else that's been going on the cupboards are bare. The kids had ice lollies and marmite on toast for lunch."

"Sounds great." He could feel a flush trickling up his neck. "The thing is, I wanted to ask you something. It's kind of important."

At that moment, Mary's phone started to buzz.

"Oh bloody hell, it's Stephanie. Again. I'm not going to answer it." Mary pushed the offending phone back into her pocket. "Would it kill the universe to give me five minutes' peace? I mean, I've solved two crimes this week and got several naughty people arrested. Surely that should grant me a little bit of leniency."

Walker flinched. Probably not the right time to ask his question. "You're having a bad day?"

"Bad?" Mary managed a tight smile. "Bloody horrendous. It started last night, actually with my not-so-wonderful ex-husband. And then this morning Johnny ate some 'mystery berries' from next door's garden. That was a call to NHS 24 before we worked out that they were just some unripe redcurrants. And Stephanie won't stop calling me up about the bloody wedding plans."

Walker's eyebrows jumped up his forehead. "A wedding?"

"Sorry, I forgot I hadn't told you yet. Matt and Stephanie are getting married. In less than six months. Oh, and the silly woman wants me to be Maid of Honour."

He swallowed. "Hang on a minute. Your ex-husband's soon to be new wife wants you, the ex-wife, to be the Maid of Honour at her wedding?"

"That's what I said," Mary replied, huffing a curl of hair away from her eye. "I think she thinks it's really modern of her or something. Of course, the kids are thrilled as they're all going to be page boys and flower girls and what have you. But why they felt the need to include me I have no idea."

"I guess she's just being nice," Walker suggested.

"Nice gets you nowhere. Damn, now I'm quoting Bernie Paterson. Sorry to be such a moan but I just can't believe it. I bet she'll make me wear pink. Or a dreadful hat or something."

It was ridiculous, Walker thought, but somehow in keeping with what he knew about Stephanie. Matt's new partner was a yoga instructor with a penchant for fad-diets and passive aggressive niceness. Mary had always made an effort to get along with her, but Walker didn't have much time for the woman. Thankfully they had never had to spend much time together.

"Oh god, you were going to tell me something weren't you?" Mary said suddenly. "Before I started moaning."

"It's all right. It wasn't anything important," he said, kissing her forehead. "I'll save it for another time." Definitely not the time, Walker thought. Not now.

"Thanks. What do you reckon, Detective Sergeant, pizza or fish and chips?" She kissed him full on the mouth.

"Let's do both. We can get a delivery and watch a TV show or something."

"As long as it's not *Vampyra*," Mary replied. "I reckon I've had enough of that woman to last me a lifetime."

Walker followed her into the kitchen. As he walked he put his hand to his trouser pocket and felt the reassuring outline of the small square box hiding within. The news about Matt's impending nuptials had put a dampener on his plans. But it wouldn't do so forever. Today was certainly not the right time. But for Mary Plunkett, he was happy to wait.

Afterword

Thank you so much for reading the latest book in the Wronged Women's Co-operative series. I can't quite believe we've made it to ten books. When I started writing these novels I had one aim in mind: I wanted to show that mums had more to offer the world than just, well, being mums. You would be right to assume that this stemmed from my own feelings about motherhood: that, while wonderful and genuinely the best thing I have ever done, it caused something of a crisis of self. When you become 'mum' and you give up work, like I did, it becomes your entire identity. This means that it is easy to lose yourself along the way. Just like Mary, I was clawing my own way back to having value beyond being a parent. I did it by writing books, the members of the WWC do it by solving crimes, but we are reflections of the same thing in the end.

And is that the end for Bernie, Mary and Liz? I rather think not. I'm having a little break after this book to pursue a side project (sign up to my mystery newsletter for more news on that one!) but I hope there will be another WWC novel in summer 2025.

Thank you for taking the time to read this and I appreciate you giving my wee books a chance. If you want to join the mystery/crime readers' newsletter that I send out once a month, you can find me at:

http://www.subscribepage.io/tescottmystery

Printed in Dunstable, United Kingdom